Biting Off A Tiny Portion Of The Strawberry, Beth Held Up What Remained, Playfully Jiggling It In Front Of Him.

"Would you like a taste?" she asked.

Reese looked past the fruit to her eyes. "I would."

All her best intentions of keeping herself emotionally distanced from him disappeared in a white-hot wave of desire. Placing her fingertips against his chest, she brought the half-eaten strawberry to his lips.

"Take it," she whispered, and he closed his lips over the fruit.

The air was scented with strawberries, his rain-wet hair and pure male essence. When he pulled her hips against his firm length, she took a deep breath.

"I want more than a taste," he said.

"I don't want this to be a game anymore."

"It's not," he said, before he drew her into his arms.

Dear Reader,

We all know that Valentine's Day is the most romantic holiday of the year. It's the day you show that special someone in your life—husband, fiancé...even your mom!—just how much you care by giving them special gifts of love.

And our special Valentine's gift to you is a book from a writer many of you have said is one of your favorites, Annette Broadrick. *Megan's Marriage* isn't just February's MAN OF THE MONTH, it's also the first book of Annette's brand-new DAUGHTERS OF TEXAS series. This passionate love story is just right for Valentine's Day.

February also marks the continuation of SONS AND LOVERS, a bold miniseries about three men who discover that love and family are the most important things in life. In *Reese: The Untamed* by Susan Connell, a dashing bachelor meets his match and begins to think that being married might be more pleasurable than he'd ever dreamed. The series continues in March with *Ridge: The Avenger* by Leanne Banks.

This month is completed with four more scintillating love stories: *Assignment: Marriage* by Jackie Merritt, *Daddy's Choice* by Doreen Owens Malek, *This Is My Child* by Lucy Gordon and *Husband Material* by Rita Rainville. Don't miss any of them!

So Happy Valentine's Day and Happy Reading!

Lucia Macro
Senior Editor

Please address questions and book requests to:
Silhouette Reader Service
U.S.: 3010 Walden Ave., P.O. Box 1325, Buffalo, NY 14269
Canadian: P.O. Box 609, Fort Erie, Ont. L2A 5X3

SUSAN CONNELL
REESE: THE UNTAMED

SILHOUETTE *Desire*®

Published by Silhouette Books

America's Publisher of Contemporary Romance

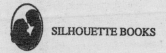

SILHOUETTE BOOKS

ISBN 0-373-05981-7

REESE: THE UNTAMED

SUSAN CONNELL

has a love of traveling that has taken her all over the world—Greece, Spain, Portugal and Central and South America, to name a few places. While working for the foreign service she met a U.S. Navy pilot, and eight days later they were engaged. Twenty-one years and several moves later, Susan, her husband, Jim, and daughter, Catherine, call the New Jersey shore home. When she's not writing, her part-time job at a local bookstore, Mediterranean cooking and traveling with her family are some of her favorite activities. Susan has been honored by New Jersey Romance Writers with their coveted Golden Leaf Award. She loves hearing from her readers.

This book is dedicated to CINDY GERARD &
LEANNE BANKS, my very own Thelma & Louise.
You took the leap and sprouted wings!

And an extra special bow to
Jim, Cathy, Linda and Candy

Prologue

"You have to do it, Beth."

"No, I don't have to do it. The idea is ridiculous, desperate and sleazy...even for you, Eugene."

"I can see where you find the task questionable. But we have to look at what's at stake here. You're being called upon to do something for your country."

"Eugene, volunteering at this homeless shelter *is* doing something for my country." Reaching across the cot, she stripped the sheet from it in one deft move. After tossing the rumpled material toward the growing heap in the aisle, she pointed to the next cot. "Want to help me here?"

Ignoring her request, the neatly dressed man clutched his portfolio to his chest, leaned closer to the smiling blonde and whispered, "For the president, Beth. Come on, think about what this could mean if you succeed. You want him reelected, don't you?"

Shaking her head in disbelief, she loosened the corner of a torn sheet. "You know I want that. But I
thought this issue of Harrison Montgomery's having
an illegitimate child was put to rest when Kelsey Gates
couldn't find proof that that cowboy, Lucas Caldwell,
was Harrison's son." Lifting the worn material from
the cot, she held it up to the light to see if the sheet was
worth mending. Her gaze darted to the man next to
her. "Eugene, don't look at me that way. I've known
Kelsey since our days at Northwestern, and if there was
anything of substance to sink her teeth into, she
wouldn't have let go until she had her story on the front
page of the *Los Angeles Times*."

Pursing his lips and shaking his head, Eugene
Sprague stared alternately at the sheet and the woman
holding it. Bundling up the sheet, Beth tossed it in the
discard pile before turning her full attention to the man
dogging her. "And don't try intimidating me with your
patronizing expression. I do care about getting President Pierson reelected and you know it."

"I'm not questioning your dedication. But if you
think sorting sheets in a shelter is the best you can do
to help your country... well, you're not living up to
your potential. Besides, how can you stand working so
many hours in this place?" He leaned forward again,
this time pushing aside her shoulder-length curtain of
curly hair. "It stinks in here."

Taking a quick look down the rows of cots, she con-
cluded that none of the people who occupied them had
heard him. "Don't you think I know that?" she asked,
grabbing him by the lapel. "Don't you think *they* know
that?"

"All right, all right," he said, avoiding her boiling
gaze. "You shouldn't take things so personally, Beth."

"Somebody has to take this personally," she said as the sense of injustice burned in her stomach. "And before you trip over that glib tongue of yours again, I think you should know that I spent a part of my childhood in places like this. They didn't smell any better then, either."

"I know all about your childhood," he said, peeling her fingers from his suit. "I also know about your life now. And you can spare the time for what needs to be done."

Eugene Sprague's practiced smile and relentless attitude got him in and out of problem situations with the majority of women on President Tyler Pierson's reelection staff. But not with Beth. She gave him a look that would have leveled most men.

Smoothing his lapel, Eugene shrugged. "You knew when you came to work for us that your life would be under scrutiny. The security of the president comes first."

Planting her fists on her hips, she stared at the president's campaign manager. "I understand the need for the initial checks into my background, but what's snooping into my private life now got to do with President Pierson's security?"

"Calm down. We tried checking into your private life," he said evenly as he looked around the cavernous room. "But you don't have one."

She shoved a hand into the soft tangle of curls touching her shoulder and shifted her stare up to the rafters. Just when she thought she'd come to terms with her past, she felt the shame creeping back in. Why couldn't she manage to put the memories of her childhood behind her and make a life for herself? Dammit, she'd been in her Bethesda apartment for six months and she was still living out of boxes. Here she was, a college-educated, twenty-seven-year-old, reasonably attractive woman making a respectable salary in a much-sought-after position on Pierson's reelection staff. Yet her goal of stability still eluded her. What was wrong? Why couldn't she bring herself to take a step toward greater permanency in her life?

"Beth? Are you with me?"

Working a stiff smile onto her face, she lowered her hand as she turned to the man in the three-piece Armani suit.

"Get real, Eugene," she said, tucking her T-shirt into her jeans. "What's flying me off to the French Riviera to chase after some playboy going to accomplish?"

"I don't believe he's just some playboy. Ever since your reporter friend got us excited over her cowboy, my people have been working day and night on the old rumor about Montgomery and his French mistress. Beth, if this rumor is true and you can prove Reese Marchand is Montgomery's bastard..."

Beth winced. "And just how would I do that?"

"You're an intelligent woman. You figure it out," he said, sliding a glance over her body. "Montgomery was crazy for blondes." He shrugged. "Maybe...like father, like son?"

"I'd do just about anything to keep the president in office, but what you're suggesting amounts to—"

"I'm not suggesting anything, Beth. All I'm saying is go to the Riviera and check this guy out."

"Check this guy out?" She slapped a hand over the political slogan on her T-shirt. "And who do I look like? Jessica Fletcher? Forget it. I have work to do right here in Washington." She made a move to pass him, but he sidestepped with her.

"Let's not be hasty."

"Send someone else," she said, pushing him aside and moving down the aisle to the next cot. "Like I said, my schedule is full with my responsibilities at campaign headquarters and the hands-on work I do at this shelter. And need I remind you that that's exactly what President Pierson's been asking for," she said, pulling off the sheet and shaking it in his face. "A little hands-on work."

They both waited until a man in a tattered shirt and shabby pants walked by on his way out of the shelter. Beth glared when Eugene pressed his precisely folded handkerchief to his nostrils.

"Consider what you're being asked to do as a different kind of hands-on work," he said, his thinning patience evident in his tilted head and tightened voice. Raising his handkerchief to silence her retort, he continued, his lips barely moving as he scanned the immediate area. "Look, Beth, I know you're not going to like hearing this, but President Pierson doesn't have time to press for passage of that housing bill you're so fond of quoting from."

"But he'll make time," she said, tugging at the mattress until she'd turned it over. "Just this morning his press secretary announced—"

"Pierson's got to get himself elected to another four years in the Oval Office first. And we've got to do our part to ensure that that happens. If we fail, then you can spend all the time you like volunteering in places like this."

Laughing softly, she *tsked* and shook her head. "You're putting too much stock in last night's CNN poll," she said with a confidence she was finding harder to hold on to by the minute. "Remember what you told me when Harrison Montgomery got the nomination? You said, 'This campaign is no longer a sailing cruise. We'll be riding a roller coaster. But never fear. We'll arrive at the end the way we started out, in the first car. All you have to do is hold on and—'"

Eugene Sprague dropped his pricey leather case to the cot and took hold of her elbows. "Listen, do I have to spell it out for you? The campaign's in trouble. Big trouble. And if we don't turn up something substantial on golden boy Montgomery soon, you can kiss that housing bill goodbye, because *he* sure as hell isn't going to come through for it."

The weight of his words had her weak at the knees. Fluctuating opinion polls were one thing, but when the head of the reelection campaign smelled imminent defeat, it made her head spin. Her entire life had led to this job. Every indignity she'd ever suffered, every embarrassment she'd ever endured, every leftover doubt she had about herself would be exorcised once she saw that housing bill signed into law. She lifted her gaze to meet Eugene's. He let go of her, and reached to smooth his hair, then straighten his tie.

"What the president's asking you to do isn't so different from what you're dealing with here," he said, jerking his thumb toward the pile of sheets. "Instead of some nameless nobody's dirty linen, it'll be Harrison Montgomery's."

Taking a step backward, she bumped into a cot. Shock coupled with momentum sent her downward to the bare mattress. The only words that registered were Eugene's first seven. "Are you saying President Pierson chose me? I met him once and all he did was shake my hand." She squinted at Eugene. "You're making that part up," she said, flashing him what she hoped was at least a suspicious look, and at best a challenging one.

"I don't have time to make this up," he said, unzipping his portfolio and withdrawing a bank statement with her name on it. "I know you don't believe in vacations or long weekends or even something as frivolous as a good address, but I think the budget for this assignment will prove how important this is."

"I don't know what you or the president want me to do," she protested as he pressed the paper into her upturned palm.

"You'll get a full briefing on that tomorrow morning in my office."

"The only thing I know about the Riviera is what I've seen in the movies. I don't speak French, Eugene," she said, hoping if she hurried through the reasons, she would convince him along with herself that she couldn't consider his suggestion. "I don't have the wardrobe. And I'm in the middle of setting up the northwest trip for July."

"Everyone speaks English. Your wardrobe is already being assembled. Dress size eight. Shoe size six and a half medium. Buy whatever else you need when you get there. Someone's already been chosen to replace you at headquarters. You're booked on a flight out of Dulles tomorrow evening."

Half hearing him, she looked up from the paper he'd handed her. "This is crazy. There's enough money here to buy one of these people a house. Two houses."

"What's that slogan on your T-shirt read? You Can Make A Difference? Well, Beth, you *can* make a difference. But not by nickel and diming away your time

in a place like this.'' Sitting down beside her, he placed
a reassuring hand over hers and spoke in a voice suspiciously reminiscent of President Pierson's own
Southern drawl. "If not you, Beth, who?"

One

" 'Never gamble what you can't afford to lose.' Isn't that what you always tell me when I come to Monte Carlo?"

Reese Marchand's searching glance around the glittering casino came to an abrupt halt on his friend. "Always," he said, absently tapping the stack of chips in his hand. "What's the matter, Duncan? Baccarat's not your game tonight?" Even as Reese spoke, his gaze began straying from his friend's frown to the entrance of the private gambling salon.

Duncan Vanos patted his empty pockets as he reached the roulette table. "Baccarat's never my game. It's your game. Remember that time in Las Vegas?" Duncan shook his head, his words dissolving into a chuckle. "She'll be along any minute now."

Reese never took his gaze from the entrance. "Who are you talking about?" he asked, bluffing badly for his friend's entertainment. He knew exactly who Duncan was talking about. The exquisite creature who'd been ducking behind columns out in the atrium tonight. The same one who'd been trailing him through Monaco for the past three days. Thank heavens she'd left off the sunglasses and head scarf tonight so he could finally get a good look at her face. He pictured her checking herself in the tiny mirror inside her purse when she thought he wasn't looking.

He couldn't *stop* looking; that she wasn't a perfectly poised clone of every other woman in a two-mile radius had intrigued him to the point of fixation. How many stalkers, he wondered, stopped every five minutes to check their lipstick and fluff their hair? No doubt about it, the lady was on a manhunt . . . for him. His body shook with silent laughter when he tried imagining what terrible things this fine-boned beauty with the brandy-colored eyes could do to him once she had him in her clutches.

Duncan leaned closer, his voice reeling with melodrama. "The way she presses her hand flat against her tummy, then takes that calming breath just before she walks by you . . ." He gave an appreciative shiver.

Reese narrowed his eyes in sincere curiosity toward his old college friend. "You've noticed that, too, have you?"

"Along with every other red-blooded man here," he said, as he moved to Reese's side and looked toward the entrance with him. "They say she's staying at Billy Waleska's place over in Cap Ferrat while he's away."

"Is she American?"

"Do you really need to ask?"

No, he didn't. If there was one thing he could always recognize it was anything or anyone American.

And he would happily bet his substantial night's winnings to prove it by locating the Made In America stamp on her derriere. A twist of a smile was fighting for control of his mouth when he pictured himself uncovering the evidence.

"Here she comes," Duncan said behind his fingers as he ran one down his nose. "Listen, if you decide to join forces with your mystery lady, we can have our talk tomorrow."

As the *croupier* raked in the house win, Reese frowned at his friend. "It's not going to happen."

"Come on. The thought of leaving the casino with that angel hasn't crossed your mind?" Duncan asked as they watched her slip into the crowd on the other side of the roulette table to buy her chips.

Reese watched as the other men there took a look, some less discreetly than others. He couldn't blame them. Her décolleté dress was showing off the creamy curves of her breasts to perfection, but the choker of large white pearls at her throat added that odd touch of sexuality that was grabbing at his gut. He repositioned his body against the hard edge of the table as he continued to watch her. Knowing she'd dressed with him in mind had him musing about the parts of her he couldn't see.

Duncan lowered his voice to a comical level. "I don't think she's following you around for a contribution to the Red Cross."

Neither did Reese, but that was beside the point. With each of her subtle movements, she set his blood humming. Reese tore his gaze from the beauty in the curve-caressing white silk. "I was referring to your marketing strategy for my champagne. It's not going to happen, Duncan. The timing is all wrong to start exporting it Stateside,'' he said as he turned back to where he'd seen her last. A sense of alarm shot through him when he couldn't find her in the crowd.

"The timing's perfect, Reese," Duncan insisted. "Have you forgotten? It's an election year. Anything's possible."

Duncan kept talking, stirring up private demons Reese didn't want to face. *Not now, not ever.* He plowed his fingers through the tousle of brown curly hair threatening to spill lower on his forehead. Straining, he squinted into the crowd, then rolled his eyes in protest over the state he was getting himself into. What was happening to his evening? Where had she gone? And why was it suddenly so important that he find her? He groaned inwardly. Why wouldn't Duncan shut up? Clamping a hand on Duncan's shoulder, he mugged for his friend. "I've got my mind on more immediate concerns here. Where in hell did she disappear to now?"

Duncan sighed with resignation, then quietly scanned the area. "I think your angel flew away, which is probably a good thing. Maybe now we can talk some business."

"My angel?" Laughing out loud at the thought, he shook his head. "If she were my angel," he said, stepping aside to allow someone to sidle next to him, "she wouldn't have abandoned me to you."

A slow smile spread across Duncan's face. "She hasn't," he said, subtly gesturing with his chin toward the person on the other side of Reese.

Reese turned his head for a quick confirmation, but once he locked onto her profile he couldn't bring himself to turn away. Close up, she was breathtaking, living up in every way to Duncan's designation. The mass of white blond curls tumbling loosely around her face befitted an angel, not the aloof, sophisticated woman she was trying to be. Her lovely, long-fingered, soft hands fidgeted mercilessly with the clasp on her evening bag until she'd snapped it open. He knew his blatant staring wasn't helping her nerves, but if she pulled out her lipstick and starting doing those sexy things with her mouth, he wasn't going to miss a second of it.

As the *croupier* called for bets, he continued drinking in the details of her face. Her clear, luminous complexion, thick, curved lashes, perfectly sculpted nose...and her mouth. He swallowed. Her incredible mouth with its unspoken promises of pleasures to share.

Breathing softly through his lips, he stood his ground when several players tried slipping in to place their bets. He wasn't giving an inch. After three days of trailing him, she'd mustered her courage to rub elbows and hips with him and he didn't want her bolting. Besides, he'd made a bet with himself that he would get close enough tonight to enjoy her fragrance. The blended scents of spring flowers and her feminine warmth were keeping him content.

But not for long.

The moment she started stroking one of her ribbony curls and biting softly on her lip, the sensations of her actions began replicating themselves along the length of his body. Her simple gestures were bringing to mind every erotic fantasy he'd had since puberty. As a mercy to both of them, he turned his eyes toward the roulette table. The empty square marked with a black two caught his eye, and without pausing, he set his stack of chips there. Discreet murmurs of approval buzzed around him.

Duncan leaned in. "Everything?" he whispered. "I hope your luck is better than mine."

From the corner of his eye, Reese could see her lifting her gaze from inside her bag to steal a glance at the numbered squares. The moment she located his wager she blinked, then widened her eyes in surprise.

"Well, Duncan," he said, loudly enough for all three of them to hear, "someone's bound to get lucky tonight. I wonder who it will be?"

Duncan smiled as the *croupier* spun the wheel, then tossed in the little ball. "Just find out if she has a sister," he said quietly before slipping into the crowd behind them.

She took out her chips, gave them a quick visual count, then bit down on her lip again. This time the guileless gesture tugged at a different organ. His heart. As the crowd around the table pulled closer to the action, she started to return the chips to her bag.

Don't be afraid, he wanted to tell her. *Take a chance.*

Hesitating, she looked up at him as if she'd heard his thoughts. Smiling and shaking his head, he focused on the wheel. "You'll never know the thrill until you've risked it all." If he'd known her name he would have said that, too, but in the end it didn't matter. She'd heard him.

She set her stack of chips on red three, the square next to his, a second before the *croupier* waved his hand to end the betting. Tapping her fingertips against her pearl choker, she raised her chin toward the wheel and held her breath. As her lashes began fluttering like little fans, a tiny line of concentration formed between her brows. For the moment the mystery surrounding her vanished, replaced by the kind of excitement that made her eyes shine and his heart pound. He understood this moment, this feeling, this fusion of fear and freedom, of letting go of the world that ruled you to wrap yourself in the thrill of danger. There was nothing quite like it, he thought, watching her.

As the ball tumbled down she braced her hands on the table edge and leaned toward the wheel, offering him a clue as to what she was like when a sense of urgency overtook her. And the game she didn't know he was playing with her became more meaningful to him than he'd ever expected.

As temptation poked and prodded him, he shifted his weight, first to one foot and then to the other. The impulse to touch her had him cupping his chin, then rubbing his hand against his cheek. If he leaned forward he could bury his nose in those blond curls to breathe in more of her scent. And make a fool of himself in the process.

She pushed up from the table edge, but the *croupier*'s call didn't register with Reese until he saw her eyes light with surprise.

"I won?"

"*Oui, mademoiselle.*"

Squeezing her hands into fists, she jerked them toward her shoulders and whispered an impassioned "Yyyeesss!" Without looking at him, she wrapped her hands around Reese's arm and shook him. "I won! I—I—"

"Congratulations."

Her head snapped in his direction. For one rich, rare moment, Reese focused on the only two things moving: her drop pearl earrings, his thudding heart. He smiled. He was one giant step closer to finding out who she was and what she wanted. And she couldn't do a thing about it. Then her unquenchable brandy-colored gaze turned from merely startled to purely panicked.

This is happening too fast, she seemed to say as she released his arm. *Please don't make me do this. I'm not ready.*

Before he could react, someone bumped into her, sending her against his chest. The next few seconds blurred into a heavenly tangle of blond hair and bilingual apologies. With her breasts pressed against his chest and her lips temptingly close to his, it was all he could do not to sink his fingers into her hair and pull her even closer for a kiss. The only thing stopping him was a whisper in the back of his brain telling him that he'd read her thoughts correctly. Now wasn't the time. But as she struggled to free herself from the forced intimacy, he could feel himself becoming more and more aroused.

"Careful there," he warned, curving his hands around her waist. He wanted to settle her hips away from his until he'd regained control, but she arched against him when his fingers touched the bare skin near the base of her spine. With commendable restraint, he forced himself not to massage the satiny depression. Because if he did, the situation threatened to become a lot worse. Or better. Clearing his throat he gently removed his hands and slipped into the crowd.

His exit was less than seamless, but more important, it was what she'd wanted—an end to their embarrassing situation. From the corner of his eye he saw her reaching for her necklace as her lips parted in alarm. He hesitated. Had she wanted him to stay or go? Her fingers were wrapping around her pearl choker as she strained to keep him in view. The next moment pearls were slipping through her splayed fingers and spilling down her breasts, bouncing off the table edge and arcing left and right. Half a dozen men made a mad, inelegant scramble with her to retrieve the pearls. He was several yards away when he turned for a better look. Already on her hands and knees, she didn't see him looking. Didn't see him smiling. And didn't see him stoop to pick up a pearl and slip it into his pocket.

Beth Langdon paced back and forth on the private beach below the Cap Ferrat villa. Hugging the cellular phone to her ear, she responded to Eugene Sprague's greeting with a rush of emotion. "This is the stupidest thing you've ever asked me to do."

"Beth, you give me this same spiel every time you call. Why don't you fast-forward to the good stuff. What have you been doing?"

"Skulking around Monaco in a scarf and dark glasses."

"The trick is to get Marchand to notice you. You've been there almost a week now. Aren't you any closer to making contact with him?"

Contact? Stopping dead in her sandy tracks, she glanced down at her bikini-clad body as she recalled her contact with Reese Marchand. She couldn't remember the last time she'd been embraced...like that. As awkward as the moment was, she remembered thinking how solid he'd felt, how alive she'd felt and how perfect they'd felt together. Then his fingers had settled on the small of her back and she'd lurched forward. The instant she made the move, she'd become achingly aware of his masculinity. Every inch of it.

From her breasts to her knees, every cell sizzled with the memory of her body moving against his. Animals in heat displayed more finesse! Swallowing hard, she forced her attention to the speed boat racing by on the open water.

"Hello, Beth? Are you there? Did you hear me? I said the trick is—"

"He noticed me...when I made a complete and utter fool of myself last night." Turning away from the sparkling water, she quickly continued. "And don't ask how. All you need to know is that the next time he sees me he's going to turn around and run the other way."

"I doubt it."

Why couldn't she get it through Eugene Sprague's thick skull that she wasn't suited for this job? Out of sheer frustration, she grabbed a handful of her filmy cover-up and rubbed at the intricate gold needlework decorating the edge. "You can doubt all you want, but that doesn't alter the fact that this overblown project of yours is a complete waste of money."

"Money's not a problem. Besides, I thought I'd told you that the funding came from a private source. No one's going to miss it at headquarters."

"Please!" Letting go of the material, she curved her hand over her sun hat and hunched her shoulders closer to the phone. "I told you, I don't want to know where the money came from. I wish you'd never bring that up again."

While Eugene attempted to reassure her that her trip would never be connected to Tyler Pierson's reelection campaign, she looked out to sea again. One sleek, white boat had broken away from the flotilla and was cruising outside the villa's private cove. She smiled longingly at the lazy figure-eight pattern the boat was making. That's where she'd like to be. Out on the water with the wind blowing in her hair and a bronzed hunk blowing in her ear. Away from this tawdry mess, with no place to go and all day to get there. She frowned and looked away. That delicious scenario wouldn't be happening anytime soon. She'd given her word to see this project through. If there was a chance that her participation could make the difference in getting the president reelected, she had no choice but to continue. With a sigh of resignation she interrupted the president's campaign manager.

"Are you holding back any information from me?"

"No. Why are you asking that?"

"Because your file on Reese Marchand says he spent four years in the United States, but I heard him speak last night. He doesn't have a trace of a French accent. He sounds like an anchorman on the six o'clock news back home. Are there any more surprises you've forgotten to tell me about?" Glancing out at the boat and the man steering it, she absently smoothed her thumb along the hip string of her bikini. "He doesn't have a wife stashed around here, does he?"

"What do you care? We're not asking you to marry him."

"It wouldn't surprise me if you did," she said, brushing aside her cover-up to plant a hand on her hip.

Eugene laughed. "In this case the end would justify the means, Beth, because when you consider the alternative..." His voice drifted off for a second. "Can you imagine where we'd all be if Harrison Montgomery made it to the White House? We're waging war here. Be a good soldier and tell me what you have planned for today."

The speedboat made a sudden hard turn and was heading straight for her shore. Who in the world...?

"Just a second, Eugene."

She walked ankle-deep into the water. Squinting hard, she yanked off her sunglasses as she silently mouthed, "Omigod, it's him." There wasn't a doubt in her mind that she was right. She'd been trailing Reese Marchand for several days and could pick him out at fifty yards. "He's...I mean, someone's coming. I have to go."

"I'm not done with you. Have the maid send whoever it is away."

"I can't do that," she said, hurrying back to her chair. "I gave her the day off."

"She's supposed to be there twenty-four hours a day."

Beth raised her voice. "The woman has a life, Eugene." Over his protests, she continued. "I'm hanging up now." Clicking off the phone, she dropped it into the canvas bag attached to her beach chair.

Her face and hands began tingling with alarm when Reese Marchand cut his motor and dropped anchor. When he dived over the side, she stepped behind the canvas sling chair. *What was he doing here?* Glancing behind her, she calculated the time it would take to make a run for the hill stairs. She dragged a nervous hand across her bare midriff. She'd never make it, and worse, she would end up looking like a frightened child running away from the school yard. Again. Lord, why had that old nightmare chosen to reassert itself at this moment? She pushed the memory out of her mind as Reese Marchand broke the surface and continued swimming toward her. With his every stroke her pulse tripled. And surprisingly, her daring did, too. Moving out from behind the chair, she walked a few steps away from it and waited.

When he stood up in thigh-deep water and casually shoved his fingers through his hair, she swallowed in awe. Water dripped down his broad-shouldered and beautifully muscled body, rearranging his dark mat of chest hair into a series of arrows. A part of her wanted to linger over his well-toned chest and abdomen, but those arrows kept pointing lower to his aubergine swim trunks. The wet material hung low on his hips, exposing his navel... but not his tan line. She briefly wondered if he *had* a tan line.

"Good morning. Mind if I join you?"

His baritone voice vibrated through her like a second heartbeat. The bizarre sensation made her forget to breathe for a second. He took a few steps toward her, then stopped and looked her over with sincere curiosity.

"You look startled. Have I come at a bad time?"

She shook her head until she located her tongue. "No," she finally managed when he walked out of the water. As his gaze wandered over her, she slipped off her broad-brimmed hat and held it first in front of her and then behind her. Why, why, why hadn't she burned this thong bikini and replaced it with a less revealing swimsuit?

"Reese Marchand," he said, reaching out a wet, well-tanned hand. "We shared an awkward moment together last night at the casino. Do you remember?"

"Vividly," she said, as he closed his hand gently but firmly over hers. His physicality was as powerful this morning as it had been last night, but she promised herself she wouldn't lose her ability to speak this time. From this moment forward she was going to be clever and witty and sophisticated. Really, she was. Just as soon as she thought of something to say. She looked down at his hand, still holding hers. His cool grip was strangely reassuring in the Mediterranean sunshine. As she looked up at him again, her gaze skimmed over the confident curve of his lips and the hint of dimples creasing his cheeks to lock into his relentless gaze. Far from intimidating her, the warmth in his smoky topaz eyes offered her humor, patience and an unnamed challenge. She started to return the smile, but calmly eased her hand from his when something else struck her about Reese Marchand's eyes. Whether it was their shape, their color or their intensity, they bore an uncanny resemblance to Harrison Montgomery's. She fought for a deep, calming breath as a prickling sensation zipped through her stomach.

"My name is Beth Langdon. How did you know where I was staying?" she asked, trying not to look at the stray water droplets still dribbling down his body. His muscular, masculine and perfectly sculpted body.

"Monte Carlo is a small town. Word gets around," he said, glancing toward the flower-edged steps leading up to the villa. "Have you known Billy for long?"

"Billy?"

"Billy Waleska, the owner."

"Oh, Billy." She smiled. "Yes, for quite a while."

"Then you're lovers?"

"Lovers?" She wouldn't know Billy Waleska if he'd popped up on her doorstep with a rose between his teeth and a bottle of champagne in his hands. But that was beside the point. Now wasn't the time to melt into an embarrassed mound of middle-class mush. This was Europe. More than Europe. This was southern France. "Mr. Marchand—"

"Reese," he said, his quiet response blending with the soft shushing of the sea.

"Reese." Tilting her head, she nodded in a way that she prayed made her appear unruffled. Fat chance of that. Smiling, she slid on her glasses. "If it pleases you to think we're lovers, go right ahead."

"I'd rather not," he said, in a way that made her smile disappear and her gaze narrow.

Moving away from him, she headed for the security of her beach chair. Dear Lord, where had she come up with such glib drivel? *Damn you, Eugene. What else did you conveniently forget to tell me?* Dropping her hat in the sand, she sank down in the striped canvas seat and sighed.

Following her a few seconds later, Reese took something from the tiny waistband pocket of his swim trunks. Squatting in front of her, he placed a small object in her hand.

"You dropped this last night."

She looked down and saw a pearl resting in the center of her palm. The humiliating moment when she'd lost the pearls and whatever dignity she had left came back to her in one cheek-stinging rush of recognition. "But I thought you'd left. How did you know...?"

"I don't miss much, Beth," he said, taking a leisurely inventory of her face and then her body as he stood. "Will you be staying for the season?"

Crossing her legs, she casually rearranged her royal blue, knee-length cover-up across her thighs and shrugged. "If nothing else interests me more, I will," she said, as she noticed him realize the filmy material was see-through and covered up nothing.

His gaze lingered over her, making her feel as closed in as that moment she'd been thrust against him last night. Only this time, they were inches away and all alone on a private beach in the middle of a sun-drenched morning. She squirmed in the chair. The scent of roses and the sea were mixing in the steamy atmosphere surrounding them. What happened to that lovely breeze just minutes ago? She was positively melting.

He smiled.

She melted a little more.

He leaned close and a drop of water fell from his chest and plopped on her knee. For a crazy moment she thought he was going to kiss her. For a crazier moment, she wanted him to.

"Mind if I use your phone?" he asked, reaching into the canvas bag beside her.

"Not at all," she said, but he'd already clicked it on and was punching out the numbers.

While he stood next to her, waiting for his party to answer, she stared at her toes, half buried in the sand. Men like Reese and moments like these only existed in James Bond movies. Didn't they? She pressed her lips together to suppress a giggle. She wasn't supposed to be enjoying this. Shoving her toes deeper into the sand, she tried putting his surprise visit into perspective, but making sense of the last few minutes wasn't easy. She had serious business to attend to, yet here she was dressed in a scandalously small thong bikini, listening to a drop-dead handsome man having a conversation *in French* on her cellular phone, and she was on the verge of having a full-blown fit of nervous laughter. This was unreal. What would her sister think of her lazing on this beach below her very own villa next to... him? Sliding her sunglasses down her nose, she glanced up at Reese, then shook her head. Teddy would definitely eat this with a silver spoon.

Leaning back in the chair, Beth laced her fingers across her middle and pretended to relax, while Reese continued his conversation. By the time he dropped the phone in the bag, she was certain she had herself under control again.

"Everything okay?" she asked.

"Yes. They're expecting us for dinner at ten tonight."

"They? Us?" Grasping the arms of her beach chair, she planted her feet flat in the sand. "Dinner?" Twisting her head to look up at him, she hadn't realized he was already moving away. "What are you talking about?"

"You didn't think I came all the way over here just to deliver your pearl?" he asked over his shoulder.

"I assumed that was a random act of kindness."

"Not when I was delivering it to someone as senselessly beautiful as you are."

"You know, you are a little presumptuous."

"Sooner or later one of us had to be, Beth. I'll pick you up at your front door at nine," he said, sloshing back into the water.

She was on her feet and running after him. "Hold on."

"Can't. I have a tennis match in half an hour." He kept on walking away, his powerful legs stirring the water into a churning froth of bubbles.

"What makes you think I'm going out with you tonight?"

"Because we have so much to talk about," he said, raising his voice for her to hear.

"Is that so? Like what?" she shouted as she waded in ankle-deep.

"Like why you've been following me around town for the past four days," he said, before diving beneath the surface.

Two

___

After several well-aimed spritzes, Beth thunked the crystal perfume atomizer onto the vanity, then leveled a warning look at the mirror. Under no circumstances was she allowing Reese Marchand to get under her skin again. The humiliating moment at the casino when she'd panicked at his touch should have been lesson enough. Obviously it wasn't, or he wouldn't have been able to catch her off-guard at the beach this morning and then make matters worse by leaving her standing there slack jawed and speechless a few minutes later.

"You're not seven years old anymore," she murmured as she reached for the gold watch beside the perfume. Her heart fluttered as she noted the time. Reese Marchand was due in five minutes, and she was going to be just fine. Snapping on the watch, she centered the mother-of-pearl face on her wrist, then fingered the bracelet-styled band. Expensive but understated, the watch, like the rest of the jewelry Eugene Sprague sent with her, was exquisite. When she caught the beginning of her smile in the mirror, she dropped her hands to her sides and glared at her reflection. "This is not your first visit to the county fair, Beth. This is work."

Grabbing her evening bag from the vanity, she hesitated before starting toward the front hall of the villa. Her work clothes never looked like this. Staring into the mirror again, she tilted her head and narrowed her eyes. She owned evening clothes, too, but they were all bought off the sale racks, for crowded campaign banquets and stuffy receptions. None of those clothes made her look and feel this way. This sexy. This powerful.

Mesmerized by her new image, she slowly traced the swells of her breasts above the plunging neckline of the designer dress. Turning around, she looked over her shoulder at the way the dress flattered her slender curves. The simple white lace number with the saucy kick pleat sent out sixty different messages. Demure, devastating, capable, sweet, sophisticated, ready...the list went on. All Reese Marchand had to understand was one message—she'd dressed with him in mind.

Heading for the entry hall, she felt a surge of confidence that wiped away any niggling doubt about her ability to deal with Reese. Whatever that challenge that she'd seen in his eyes was, she would be ready for it. Thrill for thrill, she would match him, and when the opportunity arose, she would do her best to surprise him. Delight him. Entice him. And maybe seduce him. When she finally gained Reese's confidence she would find a way to the truth about his relationship to Harrison Montgomery. And she would do it all, because as outrageous as it sounded, sometimes the ends justified the means. If it took the scandal of an illegitimate son to derail Montgomery's campaign, then this was one of those times.

As she entered the intricately-styled entry hall the doorbell began ringing. She reached for the door, but stopped short when her stomach began doing flip-flops. Strange flip-flops. The kind tinged with misgiving...and maybe a little guilt. What was she up against, really? According to his file, a high-society, highly successful champagne executive with stellar connections and a penchant for high-risk sports. She closed her eyes for a brief moment, then opened them to look around the pink-and-yellow hall with the wedding-cake trim. If she was going to pull off this charade with Reese Marchand, she had to put everything else out of her mind and start playing the palace princess. Now.

The bell rang again as she was opening the door. Reese had casually leaned his six-foot-plus, tuxedo-clad body against the doorjamb, crossed his arms loosely over his waist and was giving her a killer wink. At first glance, the light from the portico's lamp seemed to shine only on him. And why not? He looked as if he'd been ripped from the pages of *GQ*.

Courage.

Coaxing a tiny smile onto her lips, Beth let it linger as she gave him a slow once-over that started and ended on those smoky topaz eyes of his. His steadily growing smile told her he liked her bold stare. And then he took his turn. Slowly and with lingering intensity, he drank in every detail available to his eyes, and some, she guessed, that weren't. The moment was both mellow and electrifying, sending tiny tremors of awareness through her. As he opened his mouth, every intimate part of her quivered with anticipation.

"So, Beth Langdon, why *have* you been following me for the past few days?"

Pressing her evening bag against her collarbone, she widened her eyes and gave him the answer she'd been rehearsing all day. "Me following you? I think you were the one following me." She shook her finger at him. "It's true. Walking in the old city... along the harbor... at the Café de Paris... well, everywhere I went, there you were. Imagine my surprise when we bumped into each other at the casino last night." Smiling, she held her breath to see if he would buy it.

He didn't.

Nodding once, he stood away from the door and studied her. "That was very good," he said, pretending good-naturedly to be impressed with the way she'd fielded his question.

Off the hook for the moment, Beth let her gaze drift away from him. The confident smile she'd kept on her face suddenly disappeared when she saw the Jaguar convertible parked in the portico. "We're going in that?" she asked in a whisper of unmistakable admiration.

"We could catch a bus," he said teasingly, as she pulled the front door closed. He patted his pockets. "Oops, I don't have my schedule with me."

"I was joking," she murmured, walking past him to the car. She ran her hand along the gleaming door, then reached over and gave the leather seat a testing push. "Mmmmm." Soft as a marshmallow. Stretching, she drew her fingertips around the top of the wooden steering wheel and then along the dash. Richly grained walnut, she was sure of it. If there was ever an auto-

mobile she'd secretly coveted, this was the one. And
Reese had even selected her favorite color combination: a highly polished, deep green body with a light,
buttery tan leather interior. Braced and leaning over the
Jaguar, she thought about her secondhand car back in
Bethesda. Dented and badly in need of a paint job, the
economy model took up far less space than this one,
didn't require gourmet gasoline and in six more pay-
ments she would own it.

"Careful," he said, moving up behind her. "Stroking it like that may get it excited."

Biting back a laugh, she removed her hand from inside the car and pushed herself away. It *was* just a car,
she reminded herself. And she was after far more important information about Reese Marchand than his
taste in automobiles. Still, if there was such a thing as
a sexy automobile, Reese owned one. She turned to get
a peek at the side mirror and tapped her fingernails on
the polished exterior and sighed. There was no denying it, luxury felt awfully good. "You know, I've always wondered what it would be like to ri—"
Withdrawing her hand as if she'd been caught with it
in the cookie jar, Beth moved two steps back this time.
"What I meant to say was, I've always wondered what
it would be like to drive one of these."

Slipping his hands into his pockets, Reese kept on
watching her as he rested his backside against the car.
As much as he enjoyed her overt flirting, her unstudied reactions charmed him on a whole different level.
Removing his key ring from one pocket, he held it to
his chest. "Beth, it's time."

"Time for what?"

Rattling his keys, he tossed the ring into the air. "To
drive one. Catch."

She caught the keys somewhere near her knees. Staring at them, she adjusted the strap of her evening bag before she stood up and looked up. "Are you serious?"

"Only if you'll drive it with the top down," he said, taking her evening bag and setting it in the back seat.

She pulled in a slow, deep breath as a smile grew on her face. "Now?"

"Now. I love that word. It has such an immediate feel to it," he said, as he opened the car door and helped her into the driver's seat. By the time he'd walked around the car and gotten in on the passenger side, she'd inserted the key, started the engine and was wrapping her fingers around the walnut gear-shift knob. "Are you always this eager for a new adventure?" he asked, as he connected his seat belt.

She pumped the gas once and the purring engine roared with promise. "I am since I met you."

Adjusting the hem of her dress on her thigh, she shifted smoothly, then eased off the clutch. As the convertible rolled to the end of the lit driveway, her hair was already lifting in the breeze. Looking left, then right, she gunned the motor to a ripping roar this time. Her eyes brightened and a smile flashed across her face at the animal sound. "Ready?"

"Ready," he said, giving her a thumb's-up.

A shot of adrenaline buzzed through his veins as she pulled out of the driveway and headed toward the main road. Easing back in the passenger seat, he let out a hopeful sigh. With Beth Langdon beside him he could legitimately excuse himself from any more business talk with Duncan for tonight. Good friend or not, Duncan had to get the message soon. Reese was not going to the United States to sell his champagne. At least, not this year, when Harrison Montgomery was claiming half the sound bites on CNN. Reese rubbed his face in quiet frustration. The senator's familiar image was everywhere these days, but there was one place he could happily escape it. Turning his attention to the woman beside him, he smiled.

With her hair whipping around her head in a wild halo of spun gold, she smiled back. Her fresh, unstudied reaction delighted him beyond reason. He didn't know a thing about her, except that she appeared not to have a care in the world. And suddenly he was sharing that sentiment.

"How does it feel?" he asked, as enchanted with her as she was with the car.

"Like heaven on wheels," she said, competently shifting down when a service van pulled out from a side road in front of them.

As she slowed the Jaguar, Reese angled his body toward her. He hadn't seen anyone enjoy the simple act of driving a car as much as she was. She alternately stroked the wheel with her thumb and glided her palm along its curve. He imagined that same smile on her as a teenager with her first car. In typical American tradition, she'd probably named it.

When she began lightly tapping her fingers on the steering wheel impatiently, he nudged the side of her thigh. "Time to make a move, Beth."

She gave him a quick questioning look, then returned her gaze to the road. "What do you mean?"

"It's pretty much a straightaway for several miles." He leaned closer, resting his hand on his knee near the gear shift. "Pass the van. I'll watch you."

Maneuvering the car a foot to the left, she checked up the road for oncoming traffic.

"Clear?"

"I can see all the way to Italy," she said teasingly. Holding her hair away from her face, she added, "Now?"

Reese braced his hand on the dash close to the gear-shift knob. "Now." She steered the car smoothly into the opposite lane. "Excellent." Glancing down the road, he could see a set of headlights cresting over a rise. "You're fine, just give it more gas."

Her chin rose a fraction of an inch, the only sign of her increased concentration. He could sense her excitement and rode with it like a tail wind. "A little faster." At that moment the service van driving beside them began speeding up. Wrapping her hands more firmly around the knob, she stepped into the clutch, pulled back on the stick and missed the gear. The approaching car blinked its headlights in warning. His first instinct was to take over. "Get ready on the clutch," he said, attempting to remove her hand from the knob.

"Trust me. I've got it," she said, her voice steady, determined, her grip sure.

In that tense and vital moment, he found himself ignoring his first impulse. Something deep inside told him to let go. To trust her. He did, and a second later, she maneuvered the stick into gear, pressed down on the accelerator and slipped the car back into their lane ahead of the van. With only seconds to spare, the oncoming car whizzed passed them.

Several wordless moments passed, with only the purring motor and his thumping heart filling the silence. "*Ange polisson,* you give a wild ride," he said, before bowing his head in slightly exaggerated relief. After a respectful moment, he made the sign of the cross, then looked at her with mischief in his eyes. "I feel as if we should be sharing a cigarette." Before she could respond, he pointed to a restaurant sign partially hidden in shrubbery a short way up the road. "The answer to my prayers. We're here."

Pulling into the parking lot, she parked the car and removed the key. Tucking the key ring into his hand, she closed her warm fingers over his fist.

"*Ange pollison?* What exactly does that mean?"

"Naughty angel."

"Well, this naughty angel thanks you for making one of her fantasies come true." She smiled. "She owes you one."

Over the past few days he'd been gathering a number of adjectives to describe his mystery lady, but they all fell in line behind his newest revelation. Spirited. Beth Langdon just might be the one to help him out of his bind with Duncan. He watched as she unhooked her seat belt, then turned to face him. Planting a hand on the edge of his seat, she leaned closer. Her lips shimmered in the parking-lot light.

"Didn't scare you, did I?"

As much as he was tempted to lean over and kiss that smug little smile from her face, he wasn't going to. Not until the plan forming in his mind was clear to him. Shaking his head, he touched one of her diamond ear clips, then traced the curve of her cheek to the corner of her mouth. "I don't know a damned thing about you. Why you followed me, where you're from, anything about your background—"

"Is background important to you?"

He held her gaze steady with his, but didn't say anything for several seconds. "About that game you were playing with me last night at the casino—"

"The game I won?" she asked, cutting in again.

He shook his head once. "I'm not talking about roulette."

"You're not?"

"No, *mon ange polisson,*" he said, moving his fingertip over her lips. "When you play roulette, you play against the house. I want to know about the game you were playing with *me.*" Curving his hands around her rib cage, he urged her closer. "The one you're still playing."

"Why?" she asked, running her fingers through his curly hair, then spilling it over his forehead. "Because you don't want to play with me?"

"I do. I just want to know the rules."

Her hand suddenly stilled. "There aren't any. But if you insist, we'll make them up as we go along."

"And then . . . ?" He prompted her with a nod.

She didn't respond.

Beneath his curved hands her heart began beating faster. He was definitely getting under her skin. "Then, Beth," he said, "we'll break them. Every one of them." She opened her mouth, but before she could protest he added, "Starting now." Pulling her close, he kissed her until she groaned. He was certain the sound had its origins in heaven. Shifting in his arms, she plowed her fingers into his hair and began to kiss him back.

Three

National security be damned; she wasn't sharing this discovery with anyone. Reese Marchand was a brilliant kisser.

Catching her by surprise with a series of masterful tongue strokes, Reese had taken her from a gasp to a groan in seconds. Tingling sensations streamed straight from his mouth to every erogenous zone on her body. Without warning he gentled his advance to nibbling her lips, then just as quickly went back to lavishing his expert attention in the moist warmth beyond them. Shivering against the delicious intrusion, she fleetingly wondered how any woman could *not* respond to such thoroughness.

Of course, self-control *was* possible, but with the soft pressure of his hands around her rib cage, highly questionable. His light hold had somehow turned into a teasing challenge to come closer. But that wasn't going to happen. For the sake of her goal, she had to find a way out of this deepening maze of desire... just as soon as Reese stopped that nibbling he'd started again. Lord, help her. He was turning her into little more than a traitorous mass of dewy flesh.

His thorough and relentless technique had her toes and fingers curling, and she realized the only way she could straighten them was to return the pleasure. Generously. That still didn't account for her ending up on the other side of the console and in his lap when they finally broke for air.

His deadpan look toward the empty driver's seat and then to her in his lap ended in a slow, shared smile. Her hands drifted out of his hair and down to his chest. Beneath the fine pleats of his shirtfront she felt the pleasant definition of muscle, the steady thump of his heartbeat and the heat she'd help to generate. Without a doubt, he was the most handsome, most masculine, most desirable man she'd ever laid eyes or hands on.

As their connected gazes intensified, she knew she couldn't help herself; she had to touch his lips again. As she traced her own moisture on them, he captured her finger in a quick, soft bite. The moment lingered between them, rich and heavy with promise. Before releasing her finger, he flicked his tongue over the tip of it, and it seemed over other parts of her, as well. If he only knew what he was doing to her... she pressed her thighs together.

"I believe we broke two rules that time, Miss Langdon."

"I believe we did, Mr. Marchand," she said, as her body absorbed the vibration of his rumbling whisper. Was she supposed to fit so snugly, so comfortably against his solid flesh? Was the seduction of Reese Marchand supposed to feel this good?

Reaching up, he looped a lock of her hair around his finger, then stroked it across his cheek. "Shall we try for three?"

Was it necessary to indulge him this one more kiss? Was it wise to indulge herself? More questions were tumbling in, but she put them all out of her mind. As she brought her face close to his, the words rolled off her tongue. "I was just going to suggest that."

Her brushing kisses melted into one long and sumptuous move that left her mind spinning. Lifting her lips from his, she began to pull back. She was becoming entirely too pleased with herself and that had to stop. *Now.* Because there was such a thing as too much—

"Four?" he whispered.

"Four," she whispered, dipping her head again to swirl her tongue over his lips and into his mouth. Feeling the ridge of arousal pressing against her bottom, she twisted in his embrace and boldly deepened the kiss. As he began to squirm beneath her, any doubts about the wiseness of her act scattered in a hot haze of wanting and needing.

Without warning, a masculine voice sounded beside the car.

"If you two would quit making a spectacle of yourselves . . ."

Their eyes slowly opened to each other's. In a mirrored move, their foreheads touched before they turned their gazes toward the speaker. Beth recognized the tall, good-looking man as Reese's friend from the casino.

"This is Duncan Vanos, Beth," Reese said. "A good friend with bad timing."

"Hello, Duncan." She tried for an inconspicuous tug at her hem, but only succeeded in bringing both men's attention to her bare thigh. Playing the femme fatale in private was one thing, but cavorting like a human pretzel in a public parking lot was insane. Her spirits sank as she looked for an easy and modest way to return to the driver's seat. Putting toothpaste back into a tube would be easier. She was stuck in Reese's lap for the duration.

"No need to get up," Duncan said, as a good-humored smile spread across his face.

Without missing a beat, Reese continued. "And the lovely lady standing several discreet meters behind him is his business associate, Isabella Minelli."

Beth managed a small wave that ended in a casual rearrangement of her hair. "Hello." If she'd been caught sitting in anyone's lap other than Reese's, she would be speechless with embarrassment. Perhaps it was his humor or the relaxed way his hand rested on her hip, but his very nearness reassured her. Or did it? Perhaps she was slipping into her role more easily than she ever thought she could.

"Isabella. Duncan. This is Beth Langdon."

"Ah, this must be your misery lady," Isabella said, her face lighting as she came toward the car.

Duncan leaned into the car and in a stage whisper announced, "I think she means mystery."

"Yes, of course that is what I meant," she said. "So you must tell me, Reese. Have you solved her mystery?"

"I'm working on it, Isabella," he said, arching his brow when Beth turned his way again. He shook his finger. "Be warned, *mon ange polisson*, Duncan doesn't pay Isabella those exorbitant fees because she backs off."

"I see," Beth said, nodding. "Well, there's really no mystery. I was having some fun with Reese and I think he was having some fun with me. Of course, once I realized that he'd seen my entire collection of scarves and sunglasses, I decided to step up to the roulette table and, uh . . . start the ball rolling on our introduction."

Both men gave a friendly duet of loud groaning.

"So now there is no mystery? And I don't know why this is funny. I am disappointed," Isabella said, with a teasing pout.

"I'm not," Reese said, giving Beth a hot, secret look before turning to his friends. "Well, have you two turned into voyeurs or are we late?"

"None of your business and you're actually early. But we do have a problem," Duncan said, pointing over his shoulder to the fish mosaic decorating the entrance to the restaurant. "Isabella's just informed me she's allergic to seafood."

"Yes. Please forgive me for ruining this evening," Isabella said. "But I do not wish to . . ." Grimacing, she made a circle with her outstretched arms. "How do you say it? Blow up like a balloon and die."

"Isabella, what creative imagery! You must remember to tell your English teacher," Duncan said. His dramatic delivery had the dark-haired woman frowning suspiciously, until all four of them were laughing.

Reese looked at the couple beside his car and then at Beth as he gave her hip a secret squeeze. "Let's forget about trying to book another restaurant reservation and order in at my place. We'll catch the fireworks from the balcony."

"Sounds good to me," Duncan said, holding up both hands, "but never mind about calling in an order. We'll pick up something at Le Mah-Jong on the way. Meanwhile you and Beth can work on untangling yourselves. By the way, friend, Isabella and I expect a bottle of Château Beaumont's finest with dinner tonight."

As the two men staged a loud and good-tempered debate about what vintage would go best with beef and snow peas, Beth shared a smile with Isabella. The down-to-earth manner of Reese's smart-set friends had been a pleasant surprise and she began imagining the rest of the evening with them. With her next thought, she looked away. Guilt began picking at her insides. How quickly their smiles would disappear if they knew what she was up to with their friend. She shifted in Reese's lap. This cozy moment had to end. She had more important things to do than make memories that would one day plague her with shame.

Isabella reached out to pat her arm. "Champagne. Fireworks. Fortune biscuits. Beth, this is wonderful you are dating a Frenchman, no?"

Before Beth could respond, Duncan took the vivacious Italian by the hand and began leading her back to their car.

"Did she say biscuits?" Reese asked. "I swear, she knows exactly what she's saying." He shook with silent laughter.

But the word that lingered in Beth's mind was "Frenchman." Prickles started up her back at the sound of it; Isabella had handed her a perfect opportunity to ask another innocent-sounding question. While she maneuvered herself as modestly as possible out of his lap and into the driver's seat, she made certain he saw her look of mild confusion. Lord knew, that was easy enough to accomplish! Spending the past few minutes in Reese's embrace while engaging in pillow talk and soul kisses had caused her to lose her concentration. But she was back in the driver's seat now, both literally and figuratively. As she smoothed the sides of her dress, she concentrated on producing an exaggerated, squinty-eyed stare.

"Okay. What is it?" Reese asked, dipping his chin in undisguised suspicion. "You haven't suddenly remembered you're allergic to Chinese food, have you?"

"No, no. I love Chinese food," she said, turning toward him. "But did I understand Isabella correctly? Did she say something about you being a Frenchman?"

"*Oui, mademoiselle.* Born in Paris and raised near Épernay, France's champagne region. My family is, as you Americans like to say, in champagne."

"But how can that be? You don't have a French accent. When I heard you speak English last night at the casino, I would have sworn you were from the States."

"I went to college there. UCLA," he said, handing her the car keys. "Here you go. I'm ready for my next stress test."

She gave him a quick smile in exchange for the keys, but she wasn't letting up that easily. "You must have worked extra hard to lose your accent...every trace of it." She shook her head in disbelief. "In just four years of college?"

Shrugging again, he drummed his fingers against the dash. "It's just a knack. But it's not as handy for the family business as my Spanish and Italian."

When she started in with still another question, he dismissed it with a smile. "We'd better go. There's a

particular bottle of champagne I have in mind for dinner, but I'm not sure it's chilled." Twisting away from
her, he pointed toward the parking-lot exit. "Just make
the turn out of here past those cedars and head east. I'll
show you the way once we're in Monaco."

*I know the way. I've walked up that hill to your pink
stone apartment house ten times in the past week,* she
wanted to say as she fought the impulse to ruffle his
hair and make him smile. *What I want to know is the
reason behind your sudden uneasiness.* Looking ahead,
she quietly slipped the key into the ignition, started the
engine and began backing out of the parking space.
*And why I'm feeling guilty when all I'm doing is my
job.* Swallowing hard, she shifted into first and headed
out onto the road.

"Champagne," she said softly, but loud enough for
him to hear. "Sounds like a fun business. What exactly do you do?"

"You mean, what do I do when I'm not catching
pretty women in my arms at the casino, then popping
up on their private beaches to return their pearls?"

"I couldn't have phrased it better myself."

"I'm in charge of marketing it."

"I see," she said, then frowned. "But why don't you
call it Château Marchand?"

"The château belonged to mother's family. She had
no brothers," he said, drumming his fingers on the
door. "When she married, Philippe took it over."

Philippe, meaning Philippe Marchand, Sylvie's
husband, but if Eugene Sprague's speculations were
true, not Reese's father.

Reese cocked his head. "And what about you? What
puts an honest furrow in that pretty brow?"

She tilted her head to allow the air rushing by to dry the nervous perspiration at her temples. *Honest* furrow? Every time she opened her mouth she lied. "I own a chain of upscale decorating galleries I call Accents." As an afterthought to the cover story she and Eugene had concocted, she added, "I also do interior-design consulting." Whatever that was! This lying business could get way out of hand, way too fast.

As Reese repositioned himself in the bucket seat, she could sense the wheels turning behind those smoky topaz eyes. Looking toward her open window, she frowned into the darkness. She should have shut her mouth sooner. The last thing she needed was to encourage questions about a profession she knew next to nothing about. Her experience in the field consisted of her collection of home-decorating magazines.

"So you can walk into a place and know what to tell your clients to do to change or improve it."

"Well, it's a tad more complicated than that," she said, as her palms began to moisten.

"But with your professional experience, you can start sizing up a place's potential from the moment you see it."

Rubbing first one palm and then the other against the side of her dress, she forced herself to breathe normally. Reese was simply steering the conversation away from himself. He'd never have to see her handling a project as intimidating as an entire house or apartment. She could fake her way through this. "That's right, but specific ideas don't come until I begin to understand my client's personality, interests and life-style. Getting to know my clients is the most enjoyable part of my profession, but since I decided to expand the business, I haven't taken on a project in months."

He nodded thoughtfully. "You must be good if you're expanding your business."

"Well, Billy Waleska recently invested in my company," she said, as the lie she'd been living came full circle. "Since he was going island hopping in Fiji with his friends, he offered me his place this summer. We're discussing tentative plans to open a European branch...probably this autumn. I'll be poking around for new ideas this summer. You know, visiting the area's craftsmen and artists. Checking out decorating stores and touring châteaus. Maybe you could suggest a few places."

"You can count on that," he said, leaning back in the seat.

By the time he unlocked his apartment door and drew her inside to the marble foyer, their conversation about work was well behind them. He was teasing her about naming her first car as he shut the front door behind them.

"What's so funny about my naming her Susie?" she asked as he turned on the lights.

"How did you know to name her Susie and not Sam?"

Jamming a fist to one hip, she opened her other hand and gestured with its upturned palm. "I just knew." A second later she was bursting into laughter with him at her ridiculous response. "You never named a car?"

"No, but I named my boat. Does that count?" he asked, taking her hand in his again.

She could see his tension had vanished. If it had ever existed. Maybe she'd read him wrong in the parking lot. Maybe he just wasn't the type to suffer overly enthusiastic praise about his flawless English. Or maybe he simply wanted to get home to check on the champagne. Whatever the explanation, his grip on her hand was warm and steady, his attitude relaxed and charming and his attention totally on her. Reese was enjoying her company, and although the project didn't call for it, she was enjoying his.

"It depends on what you named it," she said.

"It wasn't Susie. Come on in."

Prickles of anticipation were zipping up her arm as he headed across the foyer toward a set of glass-paned doors. She hadn't felt this excited about entering a room since she'd attended her one and only White House function. President Pierson's formal reception for his reelection campaign staff had been held in the East Ballroom. She'd seen photos of the famous room, so the only surprises that evening were the watered-down drinks, crowded dance floor and President Pierson's hurried handshake.

Beth's lips parted as she walked in behind Reese. She'd pictured his apartment a dozen times, but never this way. With its white linen sofas and chairs, sage green plaid pillows and sand-colored rugs, she could easily have been in someone's living room in California. But she wasn't in California. She was in the Principality of Monaco in a Frenchman's apartment. A Frenchman with a taste for American things.

"You look surprised. Were you expecting something different?"

"Sorry," she said, smoothing her fingers over her waist. "I—well, I guess I'd pictured a lot of bachelor-black leather and high-tech toys."

"Oh," he said, waving his hand, "I keep those in the bedroom."

His steady gaze held a hint of a smile that made her wonder if he was aware of the spicy, sophisticated visions filling her head. Shoving her hand through the top of her hair, she glanced over his shoulder until she could pull herself together. "You're joking," she mumbled in a weak attempt to let him know she wasn't *that* naive.

"I'm joking," he said with a formal nod of confirmation.

Relieved that he wasn't carrying the joke further, she moved toward a silver trophy cup on a nearby table. In the photo on the wall above the cup, Reese and several other men were grouped around the same silver trophy. Behind them was a long, sleek speedboat. The display had been carefully put together, right down to a string of nautical flags arranged beneath the trophy. Beth tipped the silver cup to read the inscription on its side. The only swirling words she recognized in the engraving were Reese Marchand. As she looked over her shoulder, she saw he was still smiling. "Guess it says you won."

He nodded.

"So what *did* you name her?" she asked as she settled the heavy cup back on the table.

"Him," he corrected with a teasing wink. "My mother wanted me to call it *The Cork* because she said it might stay afloat with a name like that. But I named it *Untamed*."

Perfect, she thought as she tapped her fingernail on the glass-covered photo. "When you race *Untamed*..." She paused to smile at him. "Is it very dangerous?"

"It can be," he said.

He was at once enticing, seductive and dangerous. She swallowed hard as she tried, and failed, to put her growing attraction aside. "Doesn't racing scare you?"

"Of course it scares me," he said, giving her an odd little smile as he came toward her. "That's why I do it."

"I don't understand."

Cupping her chin in his hand, he kissed her lightly on her cheek. "No one does."

Her heart was stinging with every beat. Was she crazy, or had a look of desperation flashed across his eyes just then? Was there an unresolved conflict in his life so great that he would numb the pain by burying it in moments of sheer terror?

"Go ahead," he said, breaking the mood with a wink as he backed away. "Analyze my living room some more while I check on that champagne. Duncan and Isabella should be here soon."

As he left the room she found herself clenching and unclenching her hands. "Get hold of yourself!" she whispered. This slip-sliding emotional allegiance was caused by nothing more than the hormones he'd so adeptly stimulated in her. Still, she wanted to understand why he chose to put himself in harm's way for something as trifling as a trophy. Was he simply challenged to push the envelope because he was a skilled sportsman? With the bearing and the well-toned body of an athlete, that was certainly a possibility. Or was he just a reckless playboy out for another thrill?

Eugene's words rang unpleasantly in her ears: *"Don't let him fool you. His title at Château Beaumont is nothing more than that—a title. He's a rich, spoiled bastard, Beth. Eurotrash. There's no substance beneath that expensive facade. No depth."*

But Eugene was wrong.

There was more to Reese Marchand than fast cars, racing trophies and high-stakes gambling. She'd sensed it from the first moment she'd seen him. And because of that, the longer she knew him the more uncomfortable she felt about her role in the president's special project.

Plowing both sets of fingers into her hair, she paced in front of a wall of bookshelves. Whether Harrison Montgomery had fathered him or not, Reese Marchand did not deserve to be used like this. And the worst was probably yet to come. When her thoughts threatened to rage out of control, she sucked in a breath and held it until her lungs burned. There were good reasons to be here. Whatever guilt she felt and whatever bruises Reese's male ego might suffer were insignificant compared to the goal of getting President Pierson reelected. She had to stop wasting time on these moments of doubt. In the end, when she witnessed President Pierson signing that bill for decent housing, this tawdry charade will have all been worth it. In the meantime she was going to continue asking Reese questions and listening between the lines when he answered. When she sensed the time was right she would ask him point-blank if Harrison Montgomery was his father. Then she would get the hell out of Reese's life and never look back.

Ignoring the shakiness in her fingers, she skimmed one along the book spines on the shelf. His taste was as eclectic as hers. Bestselling spy novels, a popular cartoon-cat's guide to shopping, several pop-psychology books and— Her hand stopped the instant it landed on Harrison Montgomery's autobiography. Taking the book down, she stared at the cover photo. Was she imagining it, or were those Reese Marchand's eyes looking back at her? Was that hint of a dimple the pale proof that two men shared the same bloodline?

"You can borrow it if you like."

It took everything in her not to jump at his return. She made a point of slowly lifting her gaze from the cover. "No, thanks. I have a copy," she said, glancing down at the cover again before pressing it against her breast. There was definitely a resemblance.

Silence echoed in the space between them before Reese spoke. He was watching her with an edgy speculation.

"Thirsty?" He lifted the unopened bottle of champagne that had been resting against his side. "Eighty was a very good year."

"No, thanks. I'll wait for the others," she said, tapping her nails on the book cover. With her heartbeat echoing her tapping nails, she decided to test the waters. "I heard a team of political writers along with an image consultant wrote this. Most of the critics say it's little more than a fluff piece, but they've managed to keep it on the bestseller list for over four months."

He set the magnum into the ice bucket he'd placed on the bar, then turned to face her. Hesitating, he scratched the side of his head before he spoke. "It's a little more substantial than a fluff piece. He clearly states his vision for a new domestic agenda. And I thought the section about his tour in Vietnam and the way he connected it with the future of the military was very well done."

Avoiding the measuring look in his eyes, she opened the book and began thumbing through it. "What I can't understand is why he gave his diplomatic experience no more than half a chapter and two blurry photographs. Now, where were they...?" She was aware of him studying her for a moment more before he pushed away from the bar with a grunting laugh. Her breath caught in her throat. She felt a sense of excitement around him that went beyond the expected sexual pull. A dangerous excitement that continued to lure her right to the edge of sound reasoning.

"A lot of people," he began, appearing to choose his words carefully, "including my mother, were surprised by that omission. She knew him when he was in Paris."

"Your mother knew him?" she asked as he took the book and replaced it on the shelf.

"She was studying in Paris at the time."

Beth was about to ask another question, when an explosion went off outside the window. "What was that?" she asked, blinking as she looked past him.

"Something much more fun than politics."

Reese crossed the room and quickly opened the drapes. He smiled as she gasped at the beginning of the fireworks display; the girl did not disappoint. When he slid open the balcony doors, glittering sprays of colored light were already multiplying as they showered through the darkness over the harbor. She went to the rail, wrapped her hands around it and launched into a series of heartfelt "ooohs" and "ahhhs." With her upturned face and parted lips, she was far from pretending to be the sophisticated, megawealthy woman or the politically aware citizen now. The pop and boom intensified along with the acrid smell, but none of that bothered her. She was a little girl again, delighting in the magic she'd discovered in a summer night's sky.

In a moment of grace he told himself he didn't care that half of what she told him were probably lies. Beth Langdon made him feel the hope, the expectation and the innocence of his lost childhood, way back when fireworks were magic and the future was another happy promise. And while her interest in Montgomery seemed a bit too coincidental for comfort, he decided to chalk it up as just that.

"Look at that one," she whispered fiercely as he wrapped his arm around her waist. "Oh, isn't it just...no, that red one. *That* was spectacular."

As he turned her toward another display, she bumped her bottom against him. Whether her move was accidental or intentional, it didn't matter. His reaction was the same. He smiled to himself. "Simply spectacular."

"Stay and enjoy this," he said, reluctantly moving away when the doorbell rang. When he brought Duncan and Isabella to the balcony rail a few minutes later, Beth was still every bit as enthralled.

"Isn't this great?" she asked, moving toward the table where he was working the cork from the champagne bottle. "I haven't seen fireworks like these since we were living with...I mean, since I was a child and we were living outside Philadelphia."

As Reese began pouring the champagne, he watched her glance nervously around the balcony. Neither Duncan nor Isabella noticed the change in her voice or shift in her behavior. But he did. Considering what she was saying when she corrected herself, he had to believe she was hiding something connected to her childhood. How strange that they both would have shadows reaching so far into their pasts. And that secretly sharing this bond with her would inspire such tender feelings in him. He tried focusing his attention on filling the glasses, but decided that a little spilled champagne was worth it just to catch her profile outlined in fireworks.

Passing out the champagne flutes, he raised his toward the sky. "Here's to fireworks, wherever you can find them," he said, his gaze settling on Beth.

"Fireworks," the three of them replied as they all clinked glasses.

"Especially those you find in your own backyard," Beth said. Stepping closer, she touched her glass to his, then took a long sip. Like the spray of silver in the sky above them, the moment held on to its fragile beauty long enough to make a memory. Then it was over as Duncan and Isabella began opening the cartons of food and announcing their contents.

"Hungry?" he asked, when he saw her fiddling with a pair of chopsticks.

"Starving."

He leaned close, making certain his expression was solemn and his voice was low. "I've figured it all out, Beth, so you might as well confess."

Her gaze shot to his, strained and full of questions. "What do you mean?" she asked, as one of her chopsticks rolled from her fingers onto the table.

There it was again. A momentary glimmer of panic before she struggled back into her smile. He'd only meant to tease her, but she was trying very hard to keep that tight smile fixed on her lips.

"You flunked chopsticks," he said, deftly picking a bamboo shoot out of a carton with his own pair. Holding the vegetable close to her mouth, he urged her closer. "Don't worry," he said, as she held back her hair and bent down for the bite. "I won't let you starve."

His awkward angle of delivery left the vegetable dangling from her lips and she had to push it in with her fingers.

"Why are you looking at me like that?" she said, as she swiped at her chin with a clean fingertip. "Have I made a mess of myself?" She looked down at her form-fitting lace dress. "Tell me."

"Let me see," he said, leaning closer. She lifted her head and received a glancing kiss for her efforts. "A delicious mess," he said, licking his lips as he looked in the carton. "Beef strip?"

Opening her mouth, she moved halfway toward the food dangling between the chopsticks, before pausing to look up at him. The entire movement took less than two seconds, but it was the most erotic two seconds of his life. He swallowed as she curved her lips into a closed-mouth smile. "Maybe you should show me how to use these, instead," she said, holding up the pair she still had in her hand.

"Excellent idea." Setting the carton on the table, he took a deep breath and cleared his throat. "Just relax your fingers and move—" One of her chopsticks rolled from her hand and this time he caught it before it hit the floor. "Don't give up," he said when he saw her look of disappointment.

Taking back her chopstick, she moved to his side. "That phrase is not in my vocabulary." Carefully repositioning the sticks to mirror his, she nibbled the corner of her mouth and, with commendable concentration, eased the sticks into the carton.

"Heads up over there," Duncan said from across the table. "Isabella and I were discussing marketing Château Beaumont champagne in the States. She agrees, Reese. You ought to make that trip back with me at the end of the month."

"Not this summer. I've got other plans."

Isabella tilted her head in a show of disappointment. "Reese, does this mean you will miss the
Creighton-Lee Charity Ball?"

He shrugged.

"You're going away?" Beth asked, as the water
chestnut she'd managed to capture dropped back into
the carton.

"Would you miss me?" Before she could answer, he
looked up at Duncan. "I'm making a short day of it at
my office tomorrow and then I'm going up to the château for a visit."

"That'll take a week. Two if your family turns the
guilt screws." Duncan shoved a snow pea into his
mouth and chewed it thoughtfully. "Actually, this will
work out," he said, nodding emphatically. "It's a perfect opportunity for you to discuss my marketing
strategy, face-to-face, with Sylvie and Philippe." He
gestured with his chopsticks. "I don't know why I let
you jerk me around the way you do. This project can
be off and running by early autumn—"

"Hold on. I've got plans for the rest of the season,
too. I'm about to tackle a project I've had on hold way
too long. Almost four years too long."

With his brows meeting over the bridge of his nose,
Duncan stared at Reese for a full five seconds. "Oh,
no. You aren't talking about that relic of a house in the
middle of that turnip field halfway to Nice again, are
you?"

"Don't let him concern you, Beth," Reese said, as
he fed her a cashew from her carton. "It's not as bad
as my friend here makes it out to be. It's an old olive
mill up in the hills. About twenty years ago someone
converted it into a country house."

"Who lives there now?" Isabella asked.

"No one but bats and wild boars and the occasional roaming band of Gypsies," Duncan announced. "And I can't imagine why he hasn't sold it."

"Why would I do that?" Reese asked, locking looks with Beth. "I've considered using it as a weekend getaway for quite a while. When I found out Beth's a professional decorator I asked her to help me. And she's said yes. Isn't that right, Beth?"

Several seconds went by before she forced her mouth closed. They were all staring at her. If Reese didn't know better, he would have thought he'd asked her to perform brain surgery. He gave her his best help-me-out-here stare.

"Reese is right," she said as she turned to the others. "I can't wait to see this house. It sounds like a perfect location for relaxing and getting in touch with one's inner self." She carefully lifted a water chestnut out of the carton and into her mouth. She swallowed the chestnut and leaned forward with a smile. "But he has no idea what a busy summer he's in for," she said, causing them all to laugh.

Four

Reese jingled the change in his pockets as he looked out across the west vineyard. From the second floor of the great house he could see the last rays of sunlight filtering through the vines. With an impatient sigh, he took his hands from his pockets and pushed open the tall windows. The sweet, musky scent of ripening grapes wafted up to him in a warm breeze. Tempted by a familiar sound, he leaned over the sill to catch a glimpse of the spaniels chasing after the river swans. No matter what was happening in the rest of the world, summer at Château Beaumont usually had a calming effect on him. He drummed his fingers on the wooden sill. But not this summer.

One week away from Beth Langdon and he could swear he was going through withdrawal. He rubbed his eyes, then blinked them to clear his mind of her image. The attempt ended in dazzling failure when vi-

sions of Beth and her reactions to last Tuesday's
fireworks filled his mind. It was as if he had seen the
pyrotechnic display for the first time through her eyes
and loved the magic of it just as much as she had. He
laughed silently at the thought.

He'd done a fair amount of chasing and being
chased by beautiful women, but she was different.
From the moment he'd spotted her walking by his table at the Café de Paris until she'd fallen into his arms
beside the roulette wheel, she'd held his interest as if he
were a curious schoolboy again. The urge to touch her,
to make her laugh, to make love to her only grew
stronger each moment he was with her. And now, it
appeared, when he was away from her, too.

His fixed stare lost focus on the rolling hills outside
the window as he continued to ponder her behavior.
The pretty blonde with the brandy-colored eyes had a
way of pulling him into playful conversation, then
catching him off-guard with her personal questions. He
exhaled thoughtfully, then shook his head. If he didn't
know better, he would think Beth Langdon wanted
something more from him than his company between
dinner and breakfast.

Before he had a chance to think of what that something could be he heard footsteps in the hall behind
him.

"Reese, there you are," his mother said from the
doorway. "Claudine just called. She is bringing the
boys for a week in August. May I tell them their favorite uncle will be here?"

"Yes. And I'll be able to stay for a longer visit
then," he said, as he began closing and latching the
windows. As he had done too many times in the past,
he was about to disappoint his mother again. "I know

I said I would stay two weeks this time, but I've got to get back to Monaco in the morning. There's some business I have to take care of.''

Sylvie Beaumont Marchand didn't try to hide her curiosity. Instead, she walked up behind her son and wrapped him in a warm embrace. ''Is everything well? You've seemed preoccupied this visit.''

He smiled to himself as he pictured Beth. Her fast driving, her clumsiness with chopsticks, her willingness to break the rules. ''Preoccupied?'' Lifting his mother's hands to his lips, he pressed an affectionate kiss to her fingers. ''Yes, I am. And I apologize if that's cut into our visit.''

''I wasn't complaining. I simply want you to be happy.''

She paused a heartbeat longer than necessary, causing a prickling sensation across his shoulder blades.

''Reese?''

After all these years he still recognized the hesitation in her voice. He cringed inwardly at the subtle shift in tone that always warned him of the subject to come. Letting go of her hands, he waited until she withdrew them before he took a step toward the windows. ''What is it?''

''May I ask, is this to do with the marketing idea Duncan's been faxing Philippe about all week?''

''Indirectly,'' he said, relieved to know he'd been wrong for once. She wasn't going to talk about it after all. That one fact of his life that had torn at him since he was nine years old. As his shoulders began relaxing, he blew out a puff of air. ''What does Philippe have to say?''

''You know my husband has always believed in your instincts on these matters. He says it's your decision to make. But I urge you to consider the idea." As she moved around to his side, he could see her blue eyes glistening with guarded optimism. His heart sank. She wasn't talking about the champagne or Philippe anymore.

"Reese, this is a perfect opportunity for you to go to the States," she said, bringing her palms together in front of her breasts. "Maybe this time you could meet with him and talk. I know he must be terribly busy with his campaign, but things can be arranged quietly. Don't you think it's time—?"

Holding up his hands, Reese shook them with each word of his reply. "Mother, don't do this."

Pressing her lips tightly together, she backed away. After a few seconds she opened her mouth, but swallowed her words before she spoke them. She finally whispered, "As you wish."

If he wished for anything it was to call back his sharp words to her. He hadn't allowed his emotions to flare like that in a long time. Closing his eyes for an instant, he wondered why God had blessed him with a mother as kind and understanding and patient as Sylvie. She bore her frustration with a quiet dignity that put him to shame.

"Mother, this isn't your fault and it isn't for you to fix," he said, gathering the petite woman into a gentle embrace. "If Harrison Montgomery has something to tell me, he knows where I am. He's always known."

Beth sipped her mineral water from her straw before staring at her watch again. Three more hours until Eugene Sprague called her. Repositioning her bottom on the molded plastic chair, she fidgeted with her watch band. The scent of hot espresso and lemon cake hung in the air, and somewhere inside the café someone was playing a bluesy song on the piano. Sunlight spilled through an overhead tree branch, making dappled patterns on the white tablecloths. She could get through three more hours of this, she thought as she looked around her. Several tables away she spotted two movie stars getting up to leave and next to them, a member of royalty eating lunch with his pretty companion. There was no denying it—the day, the place and the people were picture postcard perfect.

Turning her attention to crumpling her straw wrapper into a tight little ball, she dropped it in the ashtray with a frown. "Just perfect," she mumbled to herself as she glanced over at the laughing prince and his girlfriend. Looking away, she smoothed her skirt beneath her thighs, tucked her hair behind one ear and sighed for the tenth time in two minutes. All right. She admitted it; she was lonely. But just because she couldn't get Reese's face out of her mind didn't mean this fidgety feeling was about him. Yes, he was charming and funny and, well, sexy didn't begin to describe him. But it wasn't as if she'd fallen in love with him! Something as important as love took time, commitment and honesty, and she was short on all three counts.

If she longed to see Reese again it was to get this project over with and get back to Washington. This achy feeling she had stemmed from nothing more than a good old-fashioned case of homesickness. And she could do something about that, she told herself as she began calculating the time difference between Monaco and Miami. Removing a newspaper from her tote, she dropped the tabloid on the table, then delved back into the bag and pulled out the portable phone. After clicking it on and punching in a long series of numbers, she heard her sister's recorded greeting.

"Theodora Langdon isn't at home . . ."

"Teddy Bear? Pick up. I know you're there." In the next few seconds she heard a receiver noisily removed from its cradle and then an answering machine switched off.

"Beth? Do you know what time it is?"

"Did I say Teddy Bear? I meant Grumpy Bear. And yes, I know what time it is. I miss you, Teddy."

Teddy gave a grudging groan. "Oh, I miss you, too," she conceded. "You've had me worried. We haven't talked in weeks and when I called your office that uppity boss of yours wouldn't give me your number. He said you're working on a special project. Bethany Marie Langdon, where the hell are you?"

"Monaco." Beth bit back a smile as she pictured the skeptical expression she knew would be on her sister's face.

"Right. And I've got a date with Brad Pitt. Really, where are you?"

"Teddy, I'm sitting at the prettiest outdoor café in Monte Carlo watching a certain prince, who shall remain nameless, playing footsie with a swimsuit model, whose name I can't remember. Would you like pictures or videos of this?" She heard her sister's sharp intake of air and then her scream of delight.

"Omigod, Beth. *Him?* You're not kidding, are you? What are you doing over there?"

The smile drained from her face as she sat up straighter in her chair. She rubbed her forehead as reality poured back into the lighthearted moment. "I'm working on something . . . important."

"And you can't talk about it, can you?"

Teddy's question sounded more like a statement, and once again Beth knew it was impossible to escape the grim truth of her mission for even a few minutes. Reese's face came into her mind and she slid lower in her chair. Loyalty and determination, respect and honesty, reasoning and reality swirled in her head like a windstorm. If Teddy had half an inkling about how much she needed to talk to her, her sister would be on the next plane to the Riviera. But her lifelong ally couldn't help her out with this. No one could. "Teddy, I...you're right. I can't talk about it."

"Beth, are you okay?"

"I'm fine, really," she said, striving to sound enthusiastic, when what she wanted to do was go to her sister's Miami apartment and crawl into bed with Teddy's stuffed-bear collection. "Listen, I talked to Mom and Dad a few days ago. How do you think they sounded?"

"They're fine. Well, Mom says they're fine, but you know Mom. Even after Dad's second stroke, she still believes he'll be walking on water again any day now."

Beth didn't miss the raw edge to Teddy's voice. Her younger sister had never reconciled the series of tragedies that had befallen the Langdon family. Teddy still believed every one of the family's setbacks was in some way connected to the company that fired her father over two decades ago. Beth wondered if one day Teddy would make good on her childhood promise to avenge the Langdon family's fall from grace.

"Anyway," Teddy continued, "I hope you're having some fun over there. You needed a change from that windowless office they had you stuck in."

"This is a change, all right," she said, glancing at the polished Mercedes pulling up across the street. "What about you and that attorney, the one who wants to make an honest woman out of you? Should I be planning a bridal shower?''

"You know the last thing on my mind is marriage,'' Teddy said with a teasing scold to her voice. "What about you, Miss Straight and Narrow? Is it true what they say about Frenchmen?''

"I don't know," she said, picturing herself in Reese's lap, then remembering his sumptuous and thorough kisses. She trailed her fingertips across her collarbone, then gave into a girlish giggle. "What is it they say about Frenchmen?''

By the time she said goodbye a few minutes later, her sister had her laughing loudly enough to cause several amused stares from the other diners. Clicking off the phone, Beth slipped it into her bag. Teddy could always make her smile, even if this one was already beginning to feel heavy on her lips. Resting her chin in the cups of her hands, she slid a glance toward the table where the prince and his girlfriend sat. He was whispering in the pretty redhead's ear and making her laugh that soft, intimate sort of laugh. The kind Reese could inspire in her with the arching of his brow or a purposely misplaced kiss.

Reaching a lazy hand toward her glass, she slid her fingers through the beads of water coating it, then flicked the drops across the table. Another lonely week to go trapped in this gold-plated paradise! Another seven sun-drenched days and sea-scented nights without his laughter, his smile, his touch. She slid her finger down the glass again, then flicked a few more drops across the table. *I can miss him a little if I want. No one will ever have to know. Besides, missing him a little isn't the same as missing him a lot.* Shoving two fingers into the glass this time, she flicked the water on her face and sighed. *Get real. You miss him so much, you ache for him in places you never knew you had!*

After finding out from her maid where Beth was headed that morning, Reese caught up with her at the Oceanographic Institute. At first he followed quietly behind her for the sheer and selfish pleasure of watching her move. He hadn't planned to play her game for so long, but when he realized the advantages of it he couldn't help himself. Every curious look, every enchanting smile, every nuance of motion were his to discover.

Her silky little skirt resembled a circular wave of turquoise water that refused to stay still. Skimming her sleek, tight thighs with each of her steps, the hem teased and flirted, but never settled for more than an instant against her golden tan. When she leaned toward the bubbling tanks of tropical fish she reminded him of a mermaid with her long, curly hair floating around her shoulders. Trying like hell to ignore his growing state of arousal, he told himself that watching her this way was fair play. After all, hadn't she followed him around town for a week? And this was a public place, wasn't it? Besides the extra strain on one of his favorite body parts, what was the harm?

His reasoning, rational mind shut down when she reached to lift her hair from her neck. Up went the hem of her calypso-tied blouse, exposing a tempting inch of flesh. He was caught between two heavens as he struggled to decide where to stare first—the erotic silhouette of her upper body or that tender, tempting inch near the base of her spine. She lowered her arms; he rolled his eyes.

Outside, after several more minutes of following her, he thought he was ready to end the game. But when she slowed down to look into a row of boutique windows, he decided to keep his distance. There was no reason to rush, he reminded himself. He was back in Monaco and she hadn't taken up with another man. Crossing his arms over his chest, he leaned against the corner of a building and drank in the way the sunlight gleamed off her shoulders.

When she kept her nose pressed against one display window for a full minute, Beth began arousing something else of his. His curiosity. He dragged his hand over his face. Next to flu shots, window shopping was his least favorite activity. Who would have guessed that he'd take this kind of an interest in watching it done? When she moved on, he checked to see what had held her attention. Of the half dozen items artfully displayed, he took a chance, hurried inside and bought the scarf. Shoving it unwrapped into his pocket, he stepped back into the street to catch up with her. She was nowhere in sight.

It took him twenty minutes of false starts, repeated backtracking and several rounds of colorful cursing until he located her at an outdoor café. This time he didn't hesitate to approach her.

"I'm much better at this game than you are," he said, taking harmless license with the truth. He wasn't about to tell her of his frantic search of the past twenty minutes.

She blinked twice, then stacked her hands over her breastbone. "You've been following me?" she asked, her whispered words preciously difficult to hear.

"All morning," he said, loving the delight in her eyes as much as the surprise.

"No. I don't believe it."

Sliding his dark glasses to the end of his nose, he gave her his best smile. "Oh, yes, I have," he said, with one determined nod of his head. He kept on watching as he turned an empty chair around, straddled it and sat down inches away from her. Thumping his hand over his heart, he said, "It pains me to think you were so engrossed in the antics of a school of gaudy fish that you never once turned my way." Removing his glasses, he placed them on the table, then pulled the scarf from his pocket. "I didn't even have to wear this to disguise myself."

He shook out the large square of silk, giving her just enough time to recognize the bright pink butterflies on a background of gold-and-tan stripes before he twirled the cloth into a loose rope.

"How did you know I wanted this?!" she said in an excited little whisper that made the two speeding tickets he'd earned returning to Monaco yesterday worth every franc. The honesty of her reaction made his heart pound. He didn't want to think, couldn't think, that what was happening to him was anything more than the exhilaration he felt with any pretty woman he wanted in his bed. Lifting the twisted silk over her head, he captured her around the neck, then leaned in close to her. She made him aware of wants and needs that he'd never known existed within him. Everything bright and fresh and beautiful shown in her smile. He laughed softly. "I followed the smudges."

"What smudges?"

"The smudges," he said, rubbing his nose against hers, "that you made on Papillon's shop window."

Her brow wrinkled as her expression began disintegrating into an embarrassed frown. Before she could complete the transition he brushed his lips against hers. Her gaze riveted on his mouth, then drifted up to meet his eyes. The moment sizzled with instant and unmistakable desire.

A second later she leaned in to return the kiss, but the rude noise of a car horn startled her and they both were laughing again. Letting go of the scarf tails, Reese twisted around for a glance toward the street. After a second he turned back to her, crossed his arms along the back of the chair he was straddling and sighed. He'd much rather watch her playing with the rolled edges of the scarf than watch the shenanigans in the street.

"I missed you," she said, her words coming out in a whispery rush of heartfelt emotion.

"Careful, *mon ange polisson,* I believe this sort of confession is admissible in court."

She kept her head down, but he could see by the color in her cheeks that she'd embarrassed herself with her outburst. He plowed his fingers through his hair in an attempt to regain control of his own emotions. He couldn't help himself—he was thrilled knowing Beth couldn't hold back her true feelings. The silence between them resonated with unnamed emotions, all of them frighteningly wonderful.

Letting go of the silk, she curved her hand around his. "I didn't expect to see you for another week. Everything's okay, isn't it?"

He nodded, feeling ridiculously complete as the warmth from her touch seeped all the way to his heart.

"Everything's fine," he said. "I had things to do back here. And, to be honest, I'm getting excited about working with you on the olive-mill house. Would you like to drive up to see it this afternoon?"

"This afternoon? Oh, I wish I could," she said, shaking her head, "but I have to be at the villa at three." She rubbed her temple and looked away. "You see, I have this business call I'm expecting—"

"Don't apologize," he said, experiencing his first doubt since approaching her. Maybe she hadn't been missing him, as he'd been missing her, every waking moment since they'd been apart. Maybe she had someone else on her mind. "We don't need to rush this. We can go another day. We have all summer."

"I can go tomorrow." She reached for his hand again and gave it a squeeze. "Reese, I'd love it if we could go tomorrow."

Her genuine enthusiasm scotched his doubts. She was expecting a phone call. What was suspicious about that? And he planned to meet with Duncan anyway. He could get that over with tonight. He rubbed his thumb over her fingers. "Tomorrow then. Now, what about lunch? Have you got plans for it today?"

"I'm all yours," she said, breaking into a radiant smile that tickled at his insides.

The moment was suddenly light and playful again. Even the piano player had changed his tune from blues to noisy ragtime. "Let's get out of here," he said, looking for a chance to hold her hand, to feel her leg brush against his, to wrap his arm around her waist and nuzzle her neck when no one was looking.

"You don't like this place?"

"Their *salade niçoise* is delicious, but if we stay here I can't get close enough to do this properly," he said, before bouncing a kiss off her parted lips. "See my dilemma?"

"Oh, I do," she said, widening her eyes to tease him back.

"I knew you'd understand. There's a restaurant up the street called Apple Pie. Their *salade niçoise* isn't great, but they do have the best cheeseburgers on the Riviera."

"Sounds perfect." Leaning her elbows on the table, she crooked a finger for him to come closer. "By the way, did you know there's a real prince sitting two tables behind you?" she whispered as she began dragging her tote bag across the table. "Don't look."

"A real prince, huh?" he asked, looking toward the table she'd jutted her chin at.

"Don't look, don't look!" she whispered frantically.

The two men smiled and exchanged waves before Reese turned around to her.

"You *know* him?"

"We play tennis every Tuesday." Reaching for his sunglasses, Reese slipped them on, then slid them down his nose. Looking over the lenses, he studied her for several seconds. "Miss Langdon, do I detect a little crush on the prince? Perhaps I could arrange a discreet introduction...for...you...." His voice trailed off when he spotted the tabloid newspaper that had been half-hidden by her bag. Sliding the paper closer, he nudged it around until he could see the headline over the familiar face. The Past Is Yet To Come, it read.

"Not me, my little sister's the one with the crush. At least, she had one on him when she was in high school. Wait until I tell her that—"

"If she reads the tabloids like her big sister, she'll probably be seeing the prince before you can tell her anything."

"I don't understand," she said, looking up from the money she was taking from her wallet.

Crossing his arms over the chair back again, Reese curled his fingers into an imaginary gun, pointed his trigger finger toward the street and pulled.

"Sorry, my brain must be in lock position. What are you shooting at?"

"Paparazzi. Look closer at that back-seat window and you'll see a couple of long lenses propped in the open space. They're taking photos of the prince." He shook his head. "I don't know how he stands his privacy being invaded like that."

She squinted toward the car across the street, then squirmed for a second or two before she looked at Reese again. "Well, he's a public person," she said, with a forced what's-the-big-deal shrug. "It goes with the territory, doesn't it?"

"Getting your photo snapped at a public function is one thing, but, Beth, having your privacy invaded in such a dishonest, such a sleazy way is unforgivable."

"Reese, before you say anything more, I know the *American Investigator* is a gossip rag, but it was the only thing left in English at the newsstand. Since I've been over here, I've missed the excitement of the campaign. I mean, watching it on television and reading about it."

Reese dropped his gaze to the front-page photo of Harrison Montgomery as he listened to Beth. No matter what his own thoughts were on this subject, the last thing he wanted to do was eat up what was left of their afternoon together with an argument. Unfortunately Beth appeared eager to talk about the subject.

"I was glancing at Willis Herkner's column," she said, opening to the second page. "Everyone knows the guy's a weasel, but I couldn't help myself. Since Montgomery took the lead in the polls, Herkner started writing a series of these what-if? articles." Angling the paper toward Reese, she tapped the full-page piece with her fingers. "There's probably not a grain of truth in any part of this one, but he insists Montgomery has a deep, dark secret in his past and it's only a matter of time before it surfaces."

Reese closed the paper, folded it and stuffed it in her tote bag. "And closer to the election, Herkner will be writing the same sort of nonsense about your President Pierson," he said, pushing up from his chair.

"My President Pierson?" she asked, staring up at him with a startled expression on her face. "Why did you call him that?"

"Well, you're the American here. He's your president, not mine."

"Of course," she said, brushing a lock of hair behind her shoulder. "You sound so American, I keep forgetting you're not one," she said, slipping money under her glass. "But since you lived in the States you must be a little curious about the candidates. Have you been following the race at all?"

"Off and on," he said, feeling a tightening sensation in his gut again. What would she think if she knew he'd been following the race since the moment Harrison Montgomery had announced his candidacy for the Oval Office? If she knew he tuned in to CNN four times a day, listened to political talk-radio shows in three different languages and read every article he could lay his hands on? Even rags like the *American Investigator* when he was desperate for something new. What would Beth Langdon think if she knew the deep, dark secret in Harrison Montgomery's past was an illegitimate son? And what would she say if she knew the man who stood before her, the man she was about to have lunch with, the man falling in love with her was that son?

Five

Beth, having your privacy invaded in such a dishonest—such a sleazy way—is unforgivable.

Like a sharp stone in her shoe, Reese's words stayed with her all through their bump-and-tickle walk to his favorite cheeseburger restaurant. No amount of self-indulgence made the words disappear. Nor did feeding each other curly fries, or playing all the Buddy Holly songs on the fifties-style jukebox and or even sharing a long and promising kiss when they parted a few hours later. She could no more distance herself from those words than from the guilt threatening to bring her to tears.

By the time Eugene Sprague rang her that afternoon she was pacing in front of her packed suitcases, ready to tell him she was calling off the project and heading home on the next available flight.

"Eugene, I can't keep doing this."

"Beth," he said in a crooning voice that was meant to soothe her. "I realize that you're better suited to your quiet and, shall we say, uncomplicated life back here, and that's probably what's making you uncomfortable around a character like Marchand, but—"

Slamming her hand on the antique writing desk, Beth didn't hesitate to cut off her boss in midsentence. "What I'm not comfortable with is the sneaky, underhanded game I'm playing with this man. He trusts me!"

"You're sniveling about your conscience now that you've finally got him to trust you?" he asked, his voice edging on impatience. "Take a pill."

"But I do have a conscience. A pill isn't going to help that."

"Well, you knew you'd have to sacrifice something to get this job done. If it's your conscience, so be it."

"It's not as simple as that. Whether Harrison Montgomery is or isn't his father has nothing to do with who Reese is. In case you've forgotten, none of us gets to choose our parents. Why should he be forced to pay for their indiscretion?"

"Can the sermonette. Do you honestly believe Marchand is going to lose his high-society status in that sophisticated world he plays in if it's found out his bloodlines are a little more interesting than everyone thought? Get with the program, Beth. No matter what we think of Harrison Montgomery as a presidential candidate he's the second most interesting man on the face of the earth right now. Reese Marchand will probably thank you for giving his bored friends something else to talk about besides his vulgar little racing trophies."

"You don't know anything about him."

"I'm not stupid," Eugene said quietly. "I know you and I know what's going on."

An eerie sensation skittered down her spine as she looked around the room. "What are you talking about?"

"When this is all over and you're back where you belong, I'll make sure you have some time off to sort through these doubts and see them for what they were. In the meantime, don't tangle up this project with a lot of romantic BS."

Clasping the phone with both hands, Beth eased herself into the gilt chair beside the writing desk. Had Eugene sensed something more than her plea for common decency? Well, if he had, he was wrong. Being mildly infatuated with Reese was one thing, but she'd already told herself she was not in love with him. The idea that she could be was preposterous. Unreal. Irrational.

She forced a short, sharp laugh from the back of her throat. "I'm the first to agree that he would be the perfect choice for a Monte Carlo travel ad. But if you're implying... well, don't be ridiculous."

"All right," Eugene said in a reasoning voice, "I'll take your advice. Now you take mine. Stop this nonsense and keep your eye on the bigger picture. No more skirting around cardboard boxes filled with the sleeping, freezing homeless next winter. How does that sound, Beth?"

Shifting warily in her chair, she looked toward the open terrace doors. She wasn't dumb. She knew the problem of housing the homeless couldn't go away that quickly, but getting President Pierson reelected would be a monumental step toward that goal. Her gaze settled on the lemon trees outside, their leaves rustling in the warm afternoon breeze. Beyond the garden the sea was glimmering with sunlight. "That's what I've wanted all along."

"And I have, too. I guarantee you won't be thinking about Reese Marchand when it happens. So what's it going to be, Beth? Can we depend on you to buy us a little election insurance?"

Pressing her lips together, she looked down at her hands as she clicked her nails on the edge of the desk. No matter what she thought of Eugene, she had to admit that he brought the situation back around to the clearer and more hopeful moment when she decided to be a part of the project. She closed her eyes and thought about Reese and how he would react when the game was over and the cards were on the table. Without warning, one of the last scenes in *Casablanca* played itself in her mind's eye. Humphrey Bogart's character was right; their problems didn't amount to a hill of beans.

"You can stop worrying. I'll do it. I'll stay," she said, even as she wondered how she was going to fully deal with the attraction between her and Reese. Creating emotional distance from such a compelling man wasn't going to be easy, either. "I just need a little more time and for you to stop calling me so much."

"I knew we could count on you. By the way, President Pierson's at Camp David with some of his advisers for a few days. Our press secretary's releasing a statement for the late news tonight. I don't want you getting upset when you hear it tomorrow. As a matter of fact, I want you to take it as inspiration. The president's going to need your help more than ever now."

"Why? What's it about? Eugene?" She heard a soft click. "Eugene?" Tapping the disconnect button, she stood up. "Eugene! Don't hang up!" But he already had. Cursing softly, she replaced the receiver in its cradle and went to unpack her bags.

Forget it, she told herself. Nothing mattered except her goal. Not slick Eugene and his rudeness. Not Reese's eventual reaction and guaranteed rejection of her. And not the niggling feeling that she might be going about this all wrong. The important thing to remember was she was back on track and more determined than ever to see this project through to the end.

But for all of her good intentions, she again found herself dealing with those traitorous feelings toward Reese as she glanced at him across the Jaguar's interior the next day. With the wind ruffling his hair, the morning sun glinting off his dark glasses and a half-eaten drumstick in his hand, he somehow managed to appear vulnerable to her. Squeezing the steering wheel, she looked back at the road. Control. She had to get control. He was a grown man. When this was over he'd probably roll his eyes, chalk her up as a bad gamble and try his luck again at the casino.

Before allowing another doubt to creep in, she tilted her head toward him and pointedly eyed the drumstick. "Now I know why you insisted I drive today."

"Would you like a bite?" he said, holding up the piece of chicken as he swiped at his lips with a napkin. "It's better than the Colonel's."

"No, thanks. I thought that was supposed to be our lunch."

He winked against the wind. "I had to downgrade a few pieces to brunch status when you raced by that *pâtisserie* back there. You don't know this, but their brioche is the best in all Provence."

Glancing in the side mirror and then at him, she asked, "Do you want me to turn back?"

"Miss Langdon, I have an unquenchable appetite most mornings," he said, stretching across the console. He began kissing the side of her neck. "But I very rarely turn back from anything once I've started. Feel like breaking another rule?"

With her heart skipping beats and her blood sizzling in her veins, she could barely hang on to the wheel. She pressed her body back into the soft leather seat and made herself breathe deeply and evenly as images of them making love came into her mind. When he slipped his hand under her dress and stroked his fingers across her thighs, her breath caught in her throat and she couldn't remember if she was breathing in or breathing out. "Reese?"

"Hmmm?" he said, moving his head away.

"If I crash this car, the last thing I'll remember is the smell of fried chicken." She saw his smile beneath his dark glasses.

He removed his hand from under her dress and gestured comically with it. "You American women say the most romantic things."

"We do our best," she said, trying not to giggle when he nudged her scarf away and began nuzzling her ear.

"The last thing I'll remember," he said, as his tongue grazed her ear, "is how you taste."

She swallowed a moan as they sped on through the countryside. In the background, the radio was playing a French pop song, its light melody blending with a breathy, upbeat voice. Blurred snatches of pinky purple fields and a sunshine blue sky made her feel she'd been whisked into an impressionistic painting where nothing mattered but the attention of her lover and the perfection of the moment.

Suspended from the rest of the world, she would have happily continued driving until they ran out of gas, but the song on the radio ended and a few familiar notes began. She pulled up straighter in the seat, breaking the tickling connection between his lips and her neck. "That's the international news coming on, isn't it?"

"Right," he said, pulling back in his seat and clearing his throat. "Whoa. Don't miss this turn."

"I won't." She pointed to the radio. "Could you translate for me?"

He nodded. "They're saying President Pierson is spending a working vacation at Camp David with his advisers... and that he's reevaluating the proposed housing bill... journalists had speculated he wouldn't move on it before the August recess anyway, but now they're thinking he may be backing away permanently—"

"That's not true. He'll sign it after the election," she said, shifting down to make the turn onto the narrow road.

"How can you sound so sure?" he said, settling the picnic basket more comfortably between his feet.

Accelerating again, she moved her scarf forward on her head, then pulled nervously at the knot beneath her chin. "I—well, I'm not. But funding for affordable housing has never been popular, and with the campaign heating up the issue is more politically questionable than ever." She lifted her hands from the wheel, then plunked them down again in a show of frustration. "I can't understand why, after all these years and all those hearings on Capitol Hill, homelessness is still

rampant. You'd think someone would stop being political and start . . . doing something, wouldn't you?''
She turned to him. "Well? What do you think about
that?" The back of the scarf whipped wildly in the
wind as she waited for his answer.

As Reese considered the question, his brows disappeared under the shock of hair beating against his
forehead. "I think someone next to me has a very caring and very passionate nature. Here, let me help you
with that," he said, reaching for the scarf's knot. When
he couldn't easily untie it, he slid the butterfly-printed
fabric down around her neck, then gently lifted her hair
over the back of it. "The house is down the drive on
the left, on the other side of those olive trees," he said,
sinking his fingers into her fluttering blond curls.

"Reese, I'm serious." Downshifting to make the
second turn, she looked over at him as they rode along
the tree-lined gravel. "You do agree that every family
deserves a decent roof over their heads, don't you?"

Reese shrugged, feeling mildly perplexed at her insistent tone. He formed a frown on one side of his
mouth and stared out at the olive trees. "Of course,"
he said, as she quietly parked beside the stone wall.
When he looked up at her she'd removed her sunglasses and was staring at the sprawling, ocher stone
structure as if she'd stumbled upon the Holy Grail. Either that or at the biggest challenge of her decorating
career. He wasn't sure which, but the converted olive
mill that he'd ignored for years was having an instant
and stunning effect on her.

He winced as his next thought hit him. Of course she
would be impassioned by the housing issue; her business revolved around houses. As she got slowly out of

the car, he gave the place a quick once-over, then sighed. Wait until she got a good look at this one.

"I haven't been over here in quite a while. You know, it was built in the fifteenth century," he said, feeling an unexpected need to explain the untended building and the grounds surrounding it. As he stepped out of the car, he took a longer look. Lush, shaggy vines covered the north side, all the visible wood trim needed painting and the only recognizable flowers were the white roses rambling wildly along the low stone wall. "I gave the place over to a rental management company right after I came into possession of it. I haven't been inside in a good three years."

She kept on staring at the house as she shook her head. "You bought this place without intending to live in it?"

He could already hear the gravel crunching beneath her espadrilles as he reached into the car for the picnic basket and her purse. She'd disappeared around the back of the house before he made it through the gate. "There you are," he said, when he finally located her inside the grape arbor.

As she looked back over her shoulder their gazes met through lavender shadows and streams of sunlight. He would have sworn her gauzy blue dress swirled around her slender legs in slow motion when she turned to him. Deep in the velvety green bower with its tendriling vines and clusters of grapes, she reminded him of one of those dreams that ended short, leaving him happy and sad and slightly bewildered by its power. As she began walking toward him, soft thunder rolled across the hills, branding the moment in his heart forever.

She ducked from beneath the latticed top, now cracked with years of weathering and sagging with the weight of untended vines. "How did you come to buy this place?" she asked, looking at him and then west toward the town in the valley. A breeze was picking up, stirring her curls and scenting the air with warm grapes, dusty herbs and the coming rain.

"I didn't buy it."

"Don't tell me you won all this in a poker game," she said, picking up her purse from on top of the basket. As she adjusted the leather shoulder strap, the neckline of her dress slipped aside and he could see she wasn't wearing a bra. The discovery sent a shiver of pleasure to his groin.

Taking in her teasing smile, he tried hard to decipher it. Was she amused with the overly quaint appearance of the place? Inspired? Disappointed? Disgusted? "Actually, my mother gave it to me on my thirtieth birthday," he said, as they took the path through the untended herb garden toward the rear door of the house. "She was hoping that owning a piece of property would somehow domesticate me."

"I think you have to want to live in a house before that can happen."

"Is that all it takes?" he asked, surprising himself with the quickness and unguarded tone of his question. Their eyes met for an instant as they took the low, wide step up to the door.

"For some." Turning away from him, she pressed her hands against the stones framing the doorway. "Oh, they're warm from the sun," she said, sounding as if she'd discovered a minor miracle. "Feel this." Taking one hand away, she held her palm against his cheek.

That strange sensation, in his heart for several minutes now, was suddenly filling his whole body. And scaring the hell out of him. Managing a nod, he silently cursed his besotted brain. Contrary to the crazy thought he had yesterday, he wasn't necessarily in love with her. Or was he? What was happening to him? He was beginning to feel like a stranger in his own life, and all because she'd reverently touched his house. She wasn't giving it a sacred blessing for future happiness. In Provence sun-warmed stones were everywhere this time of the day. She could have been touching any building and still have had that look of wonder in her eyes. He cleared his throat noisily, assuring himself he was a rational man. He could break this spell she had him under anytime he wanted.

"Are you sure you don't want to go in through the front door? I thought there was a certain way to see a house for the first time."

"There's no right or wrong way into a house as long as you feel welcomed there." She leaned over an empty window box and cupped her hands around her face to see inside.

"I never thought of it that way," he said, touched by her matter-of-fact delivery. Thunder rolled closer as he set down the basket and reached in his pocket for the house key. Aiming it at the keyhole, he found himself hesitating to insert it. What was he so apprehensive about all of a sudden? What was he afraid of finding...or feeling once he was in there? Turning around, he stroked the back of his neck with the key and chuckled uneasily. One would think crossing the threshold into a piece of income property he happened to own was going to change his life forever. He frowned at the absurd thought. He really did need a place in the country.

"How's it look in there?" he asked, making a perfunctory strain toward the window.

"It's hard to tell."

"Shouldn't be too bad. The management company sends in a cleaning woman once a week. It's supposed to be ready to rent at a moment's notice. Listen, maybe we should have lunch out here first before—"

"Uh-uh." Pushing away from the window, she planted a hand on her hip and shook her finger at him. "You've kept me in suspense long enough. Besides," she said, pointing to the ashen clouds moving across the valley, "it looks as if we'll be getting rain soon." When he didn't move toward the lock, she moved closer to him. "This doesn't have to be difficult."

"Maybe it will be. Are you sure you know what you're getting yourself into?"

"I won't until you open the door."

"I mean, redecorating this place could take up the rest of the summer. Is that what you want?"

"Reese, I planned to check out the shops and galleries around here anyway. I'll simply be paying better attention while I'm looking for pieces for here."

"I meant, are you sure you want to spend so much of your summer with me?"

"Of course. How else will I find out what it takes to make you happy?" She raised her eyebrows to let him know she was making light of his concerns. "Shall we get to work?"

"Why do I suddenly feel as if the doctor's asked me to take off my clothes?"

"I promise, I'll be gentle," she said, reaching into her purse and fishing out an elastic tie. She grabbed up her hair, twisted it on the crown of her head and secured it. "Let's do it," she said, jerking her thumb toward the house.

Reese unlocked the door, then pushed it open. "Welcome . . . such as it is."

Stepping over the threshold, Beth turned and reached out her hand to him. In a strangely comforting way, she appeared to be the one doing the welcoming. Smiling, she wriggled her fingers. "Come on. One more step and you're home."

Picking up the basket, he took her hand and walked in. She was already quietly and carefully scanning the vaulted kitchen space curving around them by the time he'd set the basket on the counter. The noon sun streamed through the doorway, picking out strands of her hair and coating them in vibrant light. If he didn't move away from her soon, he'd be looping those strands around his fingers and kissing her again. Letting go of her, he crossed under the stone arch on the other side of the kitchen and pretended he suddenly had an interest in testing the mortar with the heel of his hand.

Beth watched him in the archway as he twisted to follow the curve of stones. The movement caused his shirt to stretch across his torso and his jeans to pull across his buttocks. Both actions worked together to define the hard muscles, masculine planes and provocative ridges of his very male body. She ran her hands over her hips and swallowed. Her breasts and belly were aching to press against him, but all she could do was stare.

"Well?" he asked, turning to face her. "What do you think?"

She blinked and rubbed her hands together. "It must be the light. People are always talking about the light

in this part of France. You know, how it inspired all
those great painters." She shook her head, hoping to
stop her rambling. "Reese, it's positively charming. I
can't believe you've ignored the place for so long. What
made you decide to redo the house now?"

She watched as he shifted his weight from one foot
to the other, then pursed his lips as he considered her
question.

"Circumstances change, time gets away from you
and... I have no idea." Reaching up, he braced both
hands near the keystone and, with a slightly bewildered look, let his gaze stray around the interior. "I
own a house I've never lived in. I've never even slept
here."

"But you will," she said. Forcing her focus away
from his Greek statuelike pose and to the architectural
aspects of the house, she walked on.

The exaggerated stone arches and vaulted ceilings
deserved the wide-eyed stare she knew she was giving
them. So did the tiled floors, the deep-set windows and
the two fireplaces. The heavy, dark furniture was another matter. The inexpensive reproductions had the
evidence of summer rentals battered into every piece.
Running her hand over a scarred chair, she sensed
confidence rising within her. She'd waited her entire life
to have a house to decorate. In her craziest dreams
she'd never imagined anything as unique or inspiring
as an old converted olive mill in the south of France.
And Reese was handing this one over to her.

"First thing," she said, turning to see him leaning his
shoulder against the stone arch, "we haul this furniture out of here. It's positively medieval, and I don't
mean in the sense of quality antiques."

"You're the decorator," he said.

She cringed. An amateur, but very inspired decorator. Moving into the living room, she turned a quarter circle on her toes, taking in most of the room and Reese's trusting look. If redecorating his house was a way to give herself a bit of emotional distance from him, then she would throw herself into it. Starting now, she decided when she spotted the massive cantilevered staircase with the balustrade.

"Let's see what's up there."

"You go on," he said, looking out the window. "I'll be there in a minute. I have to go to the car."

She followed him back to the door, then leaned out to see him hurrying up the path. Raindrops were already darkening his three-button shirt. "I think you have a spiritual connection with this house that you're trying very hard to deny," she shouted.

"And I think I have a Jaguar, with its top down, that's filling up with rainwater," he shouted back.

Laughing at the way he'd reacted to her teasing, she went back inside and climbed the stairs to the second floor. The rooms and hallway there were filled with a pearly light that drew her straight to the window in the first bedroom suite. Pushing aside a lace curtain panel, she looked down into the back garden as the sprinkling rain turned into a downpour. The light quickly took on an ethereal quality that conjured up scenes she had no business indulging in. Before she could stop them, images of children playing in the garden came into her mind. Tousle-haired children with smoky topaz eyes. Reese was there, too, standing beside her with his hand on her swollen belly. And all the emotions and feelings she thought she was beginning to suppress bounded back with staggering force.

The images disintegrated to a lace-curtained window and unadorned stone wall, causing her to look away and sigh. If this house was going to inspire anything it would be work, she told herself sternly. Real work that would ensure against moments of insanity like that one. Rifling through her purse, she pulled out a notepad and pencil and slapped them on the nightstand. The tape measure was easier to find. Kicking off her shoes, she stepped onto the window seat and began measuring windows.

When she heard Reese entering the house a few minutes later she called out, "Upstairs, first room on the right.

"Okay," she said, when she heard his footsteps in the hall, "I want you to start picturing whitewashed pine furniture in these rooms. It's light like the stone walls, but the visual texture will contrast quite nicely." Brandishing her metal tape measure as if it were a magic wand, she turned when she heard him enter the room. "We might want to consider silk-lined linen for the—look at you!" Tossing the tape measure onto the nightstand, she headed to the bathroom for a towel. "You're soaked. I thought you were waiting out the rain in the car."

"I was on my way back, when I spotted these in the field by the olive trees," he said, setting his bundled handkerchief on the nightstand.

She got in one dab at his dripping chin before he pulled off his shirt and hung it over a chair. When he took the towel and began drying himself she reached for the handkerchief and carefully untied it. "Little strawberries." She put one in her mouth and pulled off the stem. Flavor, deep and sweet, burst in her mouth. "I didn't know berries could taste this intense."

He swiped at his face and then his chest as he watched her eat another. "They're wild strawberries. They're hard to find, but once you've had them nothing else compares."

Biting off a tiny portion, she held up what remained of the third, playfully jiggling it in front of him. "Would you like a taste?"

He looked past the fruit to her eyes. His slow, sweeping gaze moved over her face and down her body. "I would," he said quietly.

And all her best intentions of keeping herself emotionally distanced from him disappeared in a white-hot wave of desire. Placing her fingertips against his chest, she brought the half-eaten strawberry to his lips. An unexpected thunderclap echoed through the vaulted room, but that didn't scare her half as much as his pounding heartbeat beneath her fingers.

"Take it," she whispered, and he closed his lips over the strawberry. She tugged away the stem, holding on to it as she watched his jaw move until he'd swallowed. The simple acts were tinged with a raw sensuality that made the empty space inside of her contract. Startled by the strength of her response, she began to lower her hand. He closed his over it, bringing it against his chest.

Rain pattered softly against the windowpane, but she could feel lightning crackling all around them. The air was scented with strawberries, his rain-wet hair and pure male essence. When he pulled her hips against his firm length she took a deep, trembling breath. Every inch of her was anticipating the promised pleasures of his body.

"I want more than a taste," he said, the timber of his voice vibrating through every feminine part of her.

She'd waited a lifetime to feel like this. To want someone like this. And to be wanted like this. This moment would never come again. And neither would a man like Reese. Stroking her fingers through his mat of chest hair, she drew the stem over his nipples as her own tightened for his touch. "How much more?"

He slid his hands up the sides of her neck, drew his thumbs along her jaw and feathered kisses across her lips. Kisses that couldn't satisfy. Kisses that made her crazy.

Taking a condom packet from his pocket, he tossed it on the bed. "Enough to break another rule."

"I don't want this to be a game anymore."

"It's not," he said, before he drew her into his arms and kissed her hard and deep.

"Tell me again," she whispered, not caring how desperate she sounded.

"It's not a game anymore," he said, slowly working the buttons on the front of her dress. "I swear it's not."

She was ready to break another rule. The one rule she'd sworn to herself she'd never break. Opening her heart to Reese Marchand. He pushed the dress from her shoulders, lowered it to her waist and began covering her with kisses. When he drew his tongue against the pebbled tip of one breast, she gasped at the exquisite sensations.

He repeated the action, then whispered against the rosy tip, "Hold it closer for me."

She cupped her breast, making a soft pillow for his lip to play against.

"The other now," he whispered.

She curved her fingers under her left breast, waiting for him to bathe its tingling tip with his warm, wet mouth.

"Reese," she pleaded, not caring if she was half-naked and sounding like a wanton.

"The way you touch yourself for me...*mon ange polisson,* you make me so hard."

He brought his lips close to her offered nipple, then teased it with puffs of air. When she began to weave her shoulders in a restless motion, he reached beneath her dress and drew a fast hand up the inside of her leg. "Open for me," he said, patting her sleek thighs.

But she was already stepping sideways, inviting a more intimate caress. His fingers skimmed over her heat, each pass across the thin material of her panties a gentle tease. Too gentle. He was one step ahead of her, yet one step behind. She swayed against him in an erotic dance, sinking closer to his touch and the pulsing sensations he was causing.

Heeding her message with a growled string of curses, he shoved aside the scrap of fabric, slipped one, then two fingers into her slick heat and stirred.

"Beth," he said, his breath hot and demanding against her throat.

She could no more deny his erotic demand than she could stop the rain from falling. Tightening around him, she felt his fingers quivering, and her pleasure began spiraling out of control. Her legs were weak when he finally took his hand from beneath her dress.

"What was that?" he asked, his voice a tempting tease.

She looked at his rain-dampened hair, shoved back in perfect disarray, his broad-shouldered, beautifully muscled body and his hungry gaze. What he'd done to her hadn't taken the edge off her desire; it had only strengthened it, along with the need to pleasure him.

"That was just a taste," she said, liking the way she boldly teased him back. Sliding her dress and panties down over her hips, she heard his sharp intake of breath. She kicked the clothes aside. "But you want more than a taste," she said, staring at the ridge of flesh pressing against his zipper.

Swearing in French this time, Reese toed off his boating shoes, then stripped off his jeans and briefs. When he took her in his arms and lowered them both to the bed, she pressed his shoulders firmly to the mattress. Starting at his jaw, she strung a trail of nibbling kisses over his chest. Errant locks hanging from her upswept hair tickled at his body like a dozen fingertips. He groaned and reached for the condom as the solid heat of his arousal pressed against her belly.

She took the foil packet from him and pushed up to rest the lush curves of her derriere on her ankles. Her feminine grace and tender touch were more of a threat than the firm grasp he expected. Halfway there, he took over the task. And then he was pressing her back against the pillows and rolling into the welcoming space she gave him. Poised at her entrance, he held back, savoring the look in her eyes. In an epiphanous instant, he realized these feelings went far beyond the physical need to wrap himself in her satin center. "Beth," he whispered, feeling a deep, desperate tugging at his heart. "You feel it, too."

"It's not a game," she whispered. "Say it's not a game."

"It's not a game," he said, desperate, so desperate to be home. Easing into her, he whispered the message. He felt her hands on his back and buttocks, urging him deeper. Faster. Closer. Pulling back, he thrust into her again. And then again. Each time now faster, deeper, closer. She was calling out his name in little whispery pants, over and over, until the sound echoed around him like ripping silk. Her breathy, erotic demands tumbled them into a soul-shattering explosion of untamed pleasure.

Too stunned to speak, they clung to each other, waiting for the world to stop spinning, yet hoping it never would. After a while he kissed her forehead, then went into the bathroom. When he came out a few minutes later he saw her by the window. She'd closed the lace curtain over it and was peering through it down into the back garden. The clouds had moved on, allowing plenty of sunlight to filter through. Fascinated, he watched quietly as she extended her arm as if she were a ballerina, or maybe just waving goodbye. Instead she ran her fingertips over the lace's botanical design, tracing patterns against the golden light. He was struck by the beauty of her silhouetted form, and that he'd been making love to her a few minutes earlier only intensified the scene's loveliness. Maybe it was the tilt of her head or the soft angle of her shoulders, but he sensed a sadness in all that sunlit perfection. He walked up behind her. "Are you okay?"

She looked over her shoulder at him and licked a tear from her lip. "How could we be so wonderful together?"

Laughing softly, he pulled her back into his embrace. "Beth, don't sound so afraid. That's the way it's supposed to be."

Holding her naked body against his own, he knew what he was in for. All the same, he couldn't resist running a hand over her hip and across her belly. He resisted the urge to repeat the move, knowing he was playing with fire this time. He'd used the only condom

he'd brought. She turned in his arms, licking away her
last tear as she looked up at him. He couldn't ignore
the heat building in her eyes again or the blood surging to his groin.

"Then let it be that way again."

Six

Of all the stupid things he'd failed to do in his life, at the moment, forgetting the box of condoms was at the top of the list. And all because he couldn't wait to see her this morning.

Then again he wasn't totally stupid. If it hadn't been for the lone condom packet in his wallet, they'd still be discussing drapery fabrics instead of submitting to this torture. It was his own damn fault. He wanted her again so badly his hands were shaking. He tried telling himself he had every reason to be satisfied with making love to her one time, but his body wasn't buying it.

"Beth, we're going to have to wait," he said, sliding his hands up her arms to rest them on her shoulders. One deep, slow breath and with a little concentrated effort, he would have himself under control. Then he would calmly explain—

Her fingers closed over his partial arousal. "It's really not too soon," she said. The soft pad of her thumb began a slow, circular motion over him.

Swallowing a gasp, he eased her hand away. "I can't argue with you there," he said, breathing carefully through his mouth, "but we have another reason to wait."

"What do you mean?" she asked, curiosity barely overtaking the embarrassment in her eyes.

"Beth, I don't have any more protection with me." He rubbed a slightly trembling hand across his forehead, forcing his thoughts away from the lingering pleasure of her touch. "I'm always careful. I never take chances. Hell, I can't remember what sex feels like without one of those things."

A few seconds passed. A few seconds when he should have been concentrating on anything but how tempting she was with her curls falling down in disarray around her shoulders, her lips still ripe from making love and those big, blinking, brandy-colored eyes taking him in. Lord only knew what she was thinking, with the obvious proof of his arousal throbbing between them.

"Neither can I," she said quietly.

Their straying gazes locked into daring stares as the moment began pulsating with wild possibilities.

"Beth?" he whispered, reaching out twice before he eased toward her to kiss her forehead. "I'm safe. There's no risk."

"I'm safe that way, too...." *Safe so long I can't remember if it's been two years or three since I last had a lover.*

"Then ... am I crazy to ask? Just this one time?"

In his fully aroused state, his sensitivity to her dilemma amazed her. Many men would probably be whispering hot words against her ear to seduce her back into bed. Reese was asking. Many men would probably be stringing sizzling kisses down her body to confuse her. Reese looked and waited. And because of his restraint, she wanted him all the more. His caring, his consideration and genuine concern touched her more deeply than he would ever know. The truth came to her as simple, strong and straight to the point as a steel-shafted spear. They had no future, but they had this moment. Surely, if she took the chance, all she would take away would be a memory. Like a precious gift, each breath, each tender caress, each exquisite second with him would be hers. Even when he came to hate her, she would have this special time forever. "Just this once."

He picked her up and took her back to the bed. As he moved a pillow behind her head, she reached to embrace him, and bumped her purse off the nightstand. He reached to right it, but she eased him back into his arms.

"It's okay," she said, sinking her fingers into his hair. Lies and secrets scurried to the dark corners of her mind, and she had to seize this moment before they came again. "There isn't time."

"I know," he said, stringing kisses down between her breasts, then across the flat, soft plane of her belly. He raised his mouth. "But I wanted this to last," he said, before his lips caressed her tender, feminine flesh.

She shuddered against his mouth. "Oh, please. Don't say that. It can't," she whispered, closing her fists on the damask bed cover. He took her pleas as his cue to hurry, because he didn't know, he couldn't understand, the real meaning behind her response. Moving over her, he penetrated and filled her in one smooth motion. The fundamental sensation of his flesh against hers sent a thrill through her body. "Reese?" No more words were needed; he understood what she was asking.

"Beth," he whispered, looking down into her eyes. "Oh, Beth, you're like satin. Warm. Wet. Perfect."

She released a trembling breath as he began to move inside her. Spellbound by his gentleness, she blinked away tears. "I can't believe how good this feels...."

"How close I feel to you..." he said, slowing his stroke to kiss her brow. "Hold me, Beth. Hold me. Just this once."

Wrapping her legs around his waist, she drew her fingers over his hips and down the backs of his thighs. Prisoners of their own pleasure, they struggled together for release. When deliverance arrived, their fullest measure of joy came in the sweet and lingering peace they shared. Long after the carnal clutches, the desperate words and the soul-wrenching shudders, they held on to each other.

After a while, he wove his fingers through hers as if he couldn't bear to break their physical bond. Rolling to her side, he kissed the back of her hand as he looked into her eyes. The moment shimmered as she waited for his smile. *Please, don't say we were stupid to take the risk. Let it go. Let me have this moment, this perfect memory.*

"I could lie here and look at you all day," he said, running a finger down her arm. He moved his hand away and hung it over the side of the mattress. "Except for when I'd be making love to you." Lifting his head, he peered down to the side of the bed. "What is this?'' he asked, lifting a small photograph from the floor.

"What?" Beth asked, pushing up on her forearm to look. "Oh, no. Give it back," she said, reaching for the picture.

"Not so fast, I want a good look first," he said, holding it out of her reach. "Now, who are these two enchanting little girls in their braids and bows and pinafores?"

The photo, taken one summer over twenty years ago, showed two girls posed on the steps of a colonial-style house. Everything appeared normal, even the gap-toothed smiles, but over the past two decades Beth had studied the photo. The smiles were brittle, the dresses were borrowed and the house was a temporary shelter for homeless families.

"You and who, your sister? The one who has a thing for royalty?"

"Teddy," she said, nodding. "Theodora Lyn and me, Bethany Marie."

When he looked back at the photo, she wiped her sweating palms on the bed cover. Why was she over-reacting? Reese didn't know the circumstances of her life that summer over twenty years ago. And he never would. All the same, she wanted him to put the bitter-sweet reminder back in her purse.

"I see frilly petticoats and shiny shoes. It must have been an important occasion," he said, holding Beth against his hip but away from his hand holding the photo.

"I—I don't remember. Let me go. I want to pick up the rest of my things. They're scattered all over the floor."

He released her, but continued to stare at the faded color photograph after she got up from the bed. "You must have been going to a birthday party," he said, touching the creased picture with his little finger. "You see, there's a ribbon-tied package in your sister's hand."

Clutching tubes of lipstick to her midriff, Beth froze as the memory came back. "Yes, I do remember now. It was a birthday party for...someone named Gloria." She waited as, bit by bit, the memory came back.

They were at the party...and Gloria was laughing...at them in their borrowed dresses. And the other children were staring and pointing...whispering behind their chubby hands. Then the outright taunting began, and so did those feelings of panic... *"Gloria said you don't live in a house—you live in your car..." "You don't belong here..." "You're dirty...you're dirty...you're dirty."*

"But we weren't," she said in a mumbled whisper.

"Weren't what?" Reese asked, still staring at the photo.

"Nothing," she said, frantically pressing a fingertip to the corner of her eye. How could an event that happened so long ago still hold the power to hurt and humiliate her? And why now, when she'd known the greatest joy in her lifetime, did this memory have to rush in and threaten it?

"Well," Reese said, placing the photograph aside as he moved off the bed and began to help her gather her things. "I know all about little girls and their birthday parties. I have three younger sisters and there were plenty of pink-frosted cakes and pretty dresses."

"There was just the two of us," she said quietly, taking the sunglasses he was handing her. "No more sisters. No brothers."

"No brothers for me, either," he said, his voice softening to a nostalgic tone as he got to his feet and sat down on the edge of the bed. "I've always wondered what that would have been like." His smile turned wistful. "You know, I never told anyone this, but it's strange how that thought still comes to me sometimes. I mean, wondering what it would have been like with an older brother to look up to or a younger one to look up to me." He shook his head. "Here I am, pushing thirty-four and thinking about brothers I never had."

"I'm sure there are other men out there...who do the same thing," she said, as the rumors about Harrison Montgomery's past came into her mind.

What if those secret babies turned out to be real?

And what if Reese proved to be one of them?

The magnitude of those thoughts left her reeling with profound guilt and a peculiar sense of hope. But she couldn't afford to have either of those feelings. She had to get a grip on things. Reaching for her hairbrush and makeup bag, she gave an impatient sigh. "Listen," she said, placing the items on the bed with shaking hands and an encouraging smile. "While I make sure this is all of it, why don't you take your shower first."

"Well, much as I would enjoy your company in there with me," he said, bending to kiss her shoulder, "I would find it very difficult to keep my hands off your soapy-wet, beautiful body." Trailing his knuckles down her spine, he let out a theatrical groan, then headed for the bathroom. "So in the interest of safety, we'll shower separately," he said, as his evenly tanned buttocks disappeared from her sight.

Turning back to the photo, she tried holding back the encroaching sense of panic. The similarities of her past and present were uncanny. Borrowed houses. Borrowed clothes. Borrowed time. The only thing she could call her own now was a memory. She didn't belong in Reese's world of multiple addresses and hyphenated names and she never would. She was plain Beth Langdon, with one big chance to do something worthwhile. More determined than ever, she knew she would manage to put this day in its proper perspective. As for those lingering questions that never seemed to get answered . . . Picking up the photo, she stared at the bewildered seven-year-old.

"After this party," she whispered, "where do we go?"

Seven

In the three weeks since she and Reese had become lovers, Beth Langdon continued to put her heart into everything she attempted. Her total dedication mesmerized him. Whether she was making love, mastering chopsticks or selecting furnishings for his house, her instincts were right on target every time. Watching her maneuvering an adjustable lamp shade in the Menton shop made him realize that no matter what she was doing she fascinated him as much as she had the first moment he'd laid eyes on her.

"Reese, this lamp is going to fit in that alcove off the living room."

"And I want a nice lamp next to where the firewood is stored because..." He worked his hands in a slow spin that invited her to finish his sentence.

"Because you have other places to store firewood. That alcove has a low window, making it perfect for a reading area. Think about it. Once you move out the firewood, there will be plenty of room for this chair and ottoman," she said, patting the piece next to her. "Built-in bookshelves would be a breeze for any good carpenter. And when the sun sets, you could snuggle down in this chair," she said, leaning to switch on the lamp, "and read by this." Straightening up, she planted her hands on her hips, raised up on her tiptoes and looked around the shop. "I saw a wonderful little Oriental rug that would work well with this chair, too. It's the blue-and-burgundy with the cream fringe next to those rocking chairs. And if..." She stopped talking, dropped her heels to the floor and slowly turned her sheepish grin toward him. "Okay, let me have it straight. I'm beginning to drive you nuts, aren't I?"

Laughing, he drew her against him and sank down on the burgundy leather chair. "Are you joking? You're marvelous at this. I've been all but ignoring that alcove and you've come up with a plan that's so engaging you've already got me thinking about what books I want to bring up there." He reached to still her hand as she ran her thumbnail along her belt. "Beth, don't be embarrassed when I tell you these things. You're a professional. You deserve every bit of praise I can heap on you." Lifting her chin, he turned her face toward him. "You know, most women who come to the Riviera are looking to be entertained, but I sensed something different about you from the start. You know how to have fun, but you work hard and you take it seriously."

"You're being too generous with your praise," she said, as she moved out of his lap to stand. Lifting her braid, she stroked the end of it across her cheek as she lowered her lashes and looked away.

The delicate movement of her hand sent his heart thumping in a purely carnal response. They'd made love only four hours ago. Why did it suddenly feel as if it were four years ago? How could he want her again so badly, so madly? Reaching out, he curved his hand around the back of her knee. "I am never too generous with you, *mon ange polisson.*"

"Reese, be honest with me. Some of this appreciation has to do with my getting Duncan off your back, right?" she asked, as he took his hand away. She walked around the chair toward another display. "I mean, if I didn't agree to help you redecorate the house he'd still be trying to get you to take that business trip to the States."

Pushing up from the cushy leather, Reese followed her over to where she was bending to roll up the Oriental rug. "Every time Duncan's in Europe, he tries to interest me in some business venture," he said, his gaze lingering on her jean-covered derriere. The baby blue fabric hugging her curves begged for a lover's touch. A soft stroke, a well-placed pat, a lingering caress . . .

"How so?" she asked, turning to look at him.

Plowing his fingers through his hair, he lifted his gaze to her face. Her exaggerated, wide-eyed expression told him he hadn't gotten away with it; she'd caught him staring at her backside. He gave her a helpless shrug that playfully said, *It's all your fault. I'm under your spell and can't help it!* "What were we talking about?"

Laughter gurgled in her throat as she pressed her hands against his chest and kissed him. "Try hard to remember," she said, wiping her lipstick from his mouth with her thumb. "You were explaining something about Duncan before you were distracted."

"Right. When he and I were at UCLA we swore one day we'd work together," he said, loading on serious weight to his voice. "He knows we'll eventually do it. He just gets a little antsy to start something when we get together each summer."

"Well, why not do it now?" she asked, as she began dragging the rug back to the chair.

"Here. Let me help you with that." Taking the rolled rug, he lifted it onto his shoulder and headed back to the leather furniture display. "Several reasons," he said, flopping the rug onto the ottoman, then unrolling the end of it. Standing back, he gestured toward the chair, rug and lamp. "You were right. Again. These are great together."

"Good," she said, beaming him a proud smile. "I'm happy you agree. But you didn't answer my question."

"The biggest reason that I'm not interested in going to the States now is that I have plenty on my plate right here. You see, there's an emerging market for fine champagnes in what used to be the old Soviet Bloc. I want Château Beaumont to be in on the ground floor, but the competition is stiff." Reaching for a potted fern, he placed it on the seat of the chair. After a few seconds, he grimaced and removed the plant. "You're much better at putting things together. Anyway," he said, turning to face her, "I've been talking with representatives from some of these newly formed countries since early June. Nuts-and-bolts negotiations finally began two weeks ago."

She studied him quietly, then shook her finger at him. "You *do* work hard. And you play hard, too. You need the olive mill house more than you realize, Reese." Taking his hands in hers, she continued staring into his eyes. "I want you to feel happy with everything in it. You should be able to walk in that door and immediately start to unwind. It should be a place for you to come to relax and reenergize, a place you feel comfortable enough in for self-reflection. And you're only going to feel these things if the atmosphere is right." She squeezed his hands. "That's why I'm taking my time with all of this. Everyone's home should have an ambience of permanency. You should be able to say, 'This is my home and I can come here and be myself. I can depend on...'" Her voice trailed off as her face began coloring to a rich pink. "I—I'm sorry," she said, letting go of his hands. "I can't imagine how I sounded just then."

Her earnest words and her passionate delivery of them moved him deeply. "You know what I think?" he asked softly.

"I'm embarrassed to ask," she said, still shaking her head. "I'm afraid I'll start running off at the mouth again."

"I think you're the one with the spiritual connection to that house. You had an instant understanding of it the moment you saw it. Didn't you?"

She nibbled at her lip as she flicked a gaze his way.

"Beth, there had to be a reason I waited this long to do something with the house, and that reason is you. I can't imagine anyone else pulling it together as well as you are. You keep discovering all sorts of values and potential that I was never aware of. I have to tell you," he said, motioning over her shoulder for a clerk, "if I didn't have a spiritual connection, or whatever you like to call it, to the house before, I'm starting to have one now."

"You mean that?" she asked, her face an intense study of profound hope and tentative pride. "You're happy with what I've done so far?"

"Hell, yes. But as wonderfully healing as you make that house sound, I have to say, I can see other uses for it, as well."

"Tell me," she said, shaking his arm. "I love that you're getting involved."

He ran his hand over the back of his neck and shrugged. "When we stay overnight up there, I sometimes find myself thinking about how I could run my Monaco office from it. You know, an extra telephone line, a fax machine and I can see myself up there a week at a stretch. Duncan does a similar thing from his place in Malibu. He limits himself to no more than three hours of business each day when he's there and—" Reese broke off to roll his eyes. Until Beth Langdon walked into his life, he'd never thought about the olive-mill house and now he was fantasizing about relocating there. That he'd actually voiced the idea amazed him. "Now who's running off at the mouth?"

"Sorry I started it?"

"No, I don't think I am," he said thoughtfully.

As she turned her smile and attention to a display of chinoiserie bowls, Reese sank back into the leather chair. While he waited for the clerk to finish with another customer he watched Beth examining the casually displayed pieces of porcelain. She had a naturally elegant presence that made him proud when heads turned in her direction, whether she was at his side at the casino, stepping out of his speedboat and onto the dock or having dinner with his friends at a four-star restaurant. But he experienced an even stronger sense of pride when he was watching her perform her everyday tasks. When she was selecting flowers at the morning market, cooking fresh vegetables for their dinner or struggling with the French lessons he gave her, she provided him with a deep and quiet joy he'd never known before.

Smiling to himself, he laced his fingers over his belt and sighed. If he had his druthers, he'd drive up to the olive-mill house and spend the weekend alone with her. Nothing else sounded as appealing as watching her walking through the olive grove looking for wild strawberries, eating dinner at that bistro down in the valley and spending the evenings making love to her. He gave a halfhearted sigh this time when he realized that wasn't going to happen. They were attending the Creighton-Lee Charity Ball Saturday night. He might have begged off from the affair, but Saturday was Duncan's last night in Europe before flying back to California. And when Beth had found out that a portion of the proceeds went to homeless shelters, she couldn't say enough about the noble cause. Besides, he was looking forward to her reaction when they walked into the Creighton-Lees' minipalace of a summer home and she saw the surprise he'd arranged for her. Reese stood up as the approaching clerk sputtered apologies in halting English to both of them.

"We'll take these," he said, waving his hand over the items they'd decided on. As the clerk began busily checking tags and writing figures onto a clipboard, Reese walked over to Beth. "Anything else?" he asked, watching her slide her fingertip across her bottom lip while she studied the bowls. Watching her touching her mouth that way reminded him of something she'd done last time they'd made love. Feeling the first stir of arousal, he instinctively moved closer to her.

She pointed to two bowls. "For the mantel in the living room. Do you have a preference?" she asked, returning her fingertip to her bottom lip. When he didn't answer, she looked up at him.

Leaning close to her ear, he wet his lips and brushed them against her. "Yes," he whispered out of the clerk's hearing range. "I have a preference. Want to hear about it?"

Her lips parted as she kept a wary eye on their surroundings. She nodded slowly, clearly aware that he was starting the game with her. Their own private teasing game that would end in wild, lusty sex once they were alone. He'd played it with her as they'd walked through the streets of Monte Carlo the other evening. She'd played it with him on his friend Theo's yacht one long, hot and endless afternoon last week.

"I can't wait," she said, lowering her lashes as her breasts began to rise and fall with anticipation.

"To strip you naked," he said, his voice dropping to a whisper.

She leaned closer. "And then?"

"Lay you on that carpet over there."

"I'd like that." She pulled on a stray coiling curl, then tucked it behind her ear. "What else?"

Taking a quick look around them, Reese pulled at the inseam of his jeans. Today the capricious game was quickly escalating into the danger zone. But that was exactly the reason they both loved playing it. Whatever else she was holding back from him, she thrilled him with her willingness to explore her eroticism for him. "And then take you for a ride."

Her gaze dropped to the thickening ridge pressing against his zipper. "On that carpet? But how would we keep it up?"

He brushed his lips against her forehead. "Magic." Smiling, he moved away.

Reese hadn't felt this way since asking his first girl to a dance at age twelve. Drumming his fingers on his balcony rail, he phrased and rephrased the question in his mind. He hadn't asked anyone to live with him since his midtwenties and the outcome had been a disaster. But Bethany Marie Langdon wasn't a spoiled twenty-three-year-old who demanded attention twenty-four hours a day. Bethany Marie Langdon was the woman he'd fallen in love with.

When he heard the distinct rustle of voluminous taffeta behind him, he pulled in a lungful of air. "There you are," he said, turning as she carefully stepped onto his balcony. He couldn't help thinking she looked like a modern-day version of Cinderella with the tight-fitting, daringly low-cut bodice of her gown showing off the swells of her creamy white breasts. The tiny taffeta roses decorating the plunging neckline sent mixed signals by adding a touch of schoolgirl charm to her drop-dead sexy look.

"I think I'm going to regret buying that dress for you."

"What!" she said, pressing the magazine in her hand to her rib cage.

He gave her a wink and a teasing smile. "Once they get an eyeful of you, I'll be lucky to have one dance," he said, as he took her hand and drew her closer. The magazine she'd been carrying crumpled between them. "What have you got there?" he asked, moving back for a look.

"It's a news pictorial on Harrison Montgomery's State Department tour in Paris. Have you seen these photos before?"

"Beth, Beth, Beth," he said, glancing at the cover, "are you reading the tabloids again?" Taking the magazine from her, he tossed it on the table, then pulled her into his lap as he sat down. "*Mon ange polisson,* you amaze me. You have the fervor of an intellectual when it comes to American politics, yet you manage to come up with one of those rags at least once a week."

"But, Reese," she said, her protest bordering on a frustrated yet comical whine. Reaching for the corner of the paper hanging over the edge of the table, she managed to retrieve it. "This one's published right here in Monaco. Or is it France? Well, it doesn't matter, because I'm still not good enough with my French to translate much. The interesting thing is that it consists mainly of photographs," she said, shuffling through the pages. She raised her brows as she inverted the centerfold, then creased the paper in half. "And I wanted you to look at one in particular."

"All right. Just one. Then we'll share a glass of champagne. I wanted to talk to you about something," he said, circling her waist and pretending to teethe on her pearl necklace. "Mmmmm. These taste better since I had them restrung." He felt her long, ardent sigh as his lips brushed her collarbone. In a matter of seconds she was twisting toward him, offering him more of her bare skin to nuzzle. When she reached to sink the fingers of one hand into his hair, the magazine crumpled between them again.

"I—I'd better not have any champagne," she said, smoothing the magazine. "My stomach's a little jumpy."

"Okay, I'll hold off until later. Are you sure you're okay? You look...different tonight."

"I'm fine," she said, "But, Reese, look at this."

He felt his heart imploding. He thought he'd seen every photo of Harrison Montgomery ever taken during his embassy days in Paris all those years ago. But not this one with his mother in it. "What do you know...there's my mother," he said, pouring on false delight. He sensed Beth holding her breath, waiting, watching. "Isn't that something? I'll have to send that to her."

"I saw the name Sylvie Beaumont under the photo along with Montgomery's. You'll have to translate it for me, but I think it says something about them attending a movie premiere."

Reese glanced at the caption, then laughed. "*Très bien*. My French tutoring's finally beginning to pay off."

Beth was as far from cracking a smile as she was from being fluent in French. Fingering her necklace, she lowered her lashes as if to draw courage for whatever she was about to do. "She was a beautiful woman."

He gave a theatrical shrug. "She still is."

"I think I figured out the dates under the photograph." As she shoved her hair behind her ears, her gaze shifted from the photo to Reese and back again. "You know, I—well, I know it sounds crazy, but it was thirty-five years ago that he was in Paris. Has your mother ever hinted that she and Montgomery had a relationship?" She frowned. "If I cover the bottom half of his face," she said, laying two fingers there on the photograph, "his eyes … it's like looking into your eyes."

Reese had sensed something like this was coming, and hoped he'd used the time wisely choreographing his response. "Is this going somewhere?" Mouth open … blink … stare … lean forward … "Me?" Laughter … pregnant pause … laughter again … "That's what you thought?" He slouched back in the chair, took the magazine from her and stared at the photo in question. Shaking his head, he said, "I've got to do something about upgrading your reading material."

"Well, you have to admit there are some similarities," she said, carefully moving off his lap.

Glancing at the magazine in his hand, he batted his eyelids furiously at it and then at her. "If you say so," he said, giving her back the magazine. Standing up, he began backing into the living room. "I left my watch in the bedroom. I'll be right back."

Beth placed the magazine on the table, wrapped her arms tightly around her waist and moved toward the balcony rail. She stood rigid and erect as she stared out over the harbor. Everything in the principality appeared in perfect order. The yachts were bobbing in their slips. A toylike helicopter was lifting off its rooftop pad. The sun was setting over the compact skyline. And all the while her heart was sitting in her stomach, numbing her blood as if it were a chunk of ice.

She knew Reese Marchand. They'd been lovers for three weeks. She knew that he slept with his forearm thrown across his brow, she knew that he liked his toast light and she knew that he'd once saved a man from drowning. She knew how to wake him up, how to make him laugh and what made his breath catch in the back of his throat. As charming and funny as his reaction had been to the photo in the magazine, she knew Reese was lying to her. She knew it as surely as she knew those other things about him. Her last doubt had vanished. Reese Marchand was Harrison Montgomery's son. The question was, how was she going to prove it and still keep her sanity?

"Reese, I was hoping we could talk privately before I left tomorrow."

Reese turned his head toward Duncan. "I think I know what this is about," he said, "and I apologize. We haven't spent much time together during your trip here, have we?"

"It's not that," Duncan said, as they both looked up at Beth dancing by them. She was in the arms of Reese's Tuesday tennis friend, the prince.

"You should have seen the surprise on Beth's face when I introduced them," Reese said, momentarily forgetting Duncan's serious tone. "She's getting quite a kick out of dancing with him."

Swirling his drink in his glass, Duncan gave him a shallow smile. "I hear his family's got him up against the palace wall to get himself married," Duncan said, slipping his other hand in his tuxedo pants pockets. He studied the floor for a moment.

"What's with you tonight? You look as if your accountant took an unexpected trip to Argentina."

Pursing his lips, Duncan brought his gaze level with Reese. "I would know what to do about him. It's Beth Langdon I'm not so sure about."

"That again. Look, Duncan, I don't want you making the mistake of connecting her with my decision not to go to the States. The timing's all wrong for that trip. When I take the Château Beaumont label west, I want my desk clear back here. And it won't be for—"

"This has nothing to do with selling champagne," he said, setting his glass on a marble tabletop. Gesturing with his free hand, he leaned toward Reese. "We've been friends for almost fifteen years and in all that time I've never seen you like this with any other woman."

"Maybe you should try sounding a little happier for me when you say that." He looked back at the dance floor, providing his friend with an opportunity to change the subject.

Duncan stepped in front of him, effectively blocking his view. "You've dated a beauty queen, a princess and too many actresses to count, but none of them could do to you what Beth Langdon's doing."

"And what's that?" he asked, pulling at his collar. "Burning up my brain cells with all that energy she generates?"

"Reese, she's beautiful, she's funny and Lord knows I hate getting into a conversation with her on anything political because I always end up feeling like an idiot. But something's not..."

"Something's not what?" Reese asked, not bothering to keep the irritation out of his voice this time.

"People have been talking."

"What the hell are you getting at?"

"Don't shoot this messenger," Duncan said, pressing his thumb to his chest as he moved to Reese's side. "I'm your friend, remember? But what's it been? Five, six weeks tops since you met her? Unless she's told you things about herself that you'd rather not share, I have to wonder how much you actually know about her."

"Just what do you think she's up to?" he asked, opening his hands and shrugging. "Come on. What's everyone worrying about? She's certainly not a gold-digging pauper. What do I have that she would want?"

"I have no idea. Maybe it's not you. Maybe she's running from something or someone and the best way to do that is by wiping out her past by creating a new one for herself. One she's not very familiar with yet."

"I don't understand what you're talking about," he said, even though he did. He used to enjoy the aura of mystery surrounding her, but lately it had begun to make him uneasy. She'd been so open, so honest about everything . . . except her life back in the States.

"Reese, the other day when we were out on Theo's yacht, I heard her mentioning to someone that one of her decorator galleries is located near Philadelphia. When I asked where, she cleverly evaded my question. Don't you find it odd that she would go to the trouble of not answering a simple question about her business?"

Reese pulled his hand from his pocket and held it up to silence Duncan. "You're blowing this way out of proportion. If there's anything worth knowing, I'm sure Beth will tell me when she's ready."

"I have family in that area. If you want me to see what I can find out about her—"

"Of course not. I wouldn't want anyone poking around my private life and neither would you. People are entitled to their secrets until they're ready to give them up."

"It's not her private life, Reese. She either owns this chain of stores or she doesn't. If the latter turns out to be true, you can take it from there."

Reese shook his head. "You'd better let this go."

The moment lingered in the air between them, potent as a toxic vapor. Then Duncan took a long, slow breath as he looked up at one of a dozen chandeliers. After a few seconds he blew out a puff of air. "Whatever you say," he said, infusing his voice with hardy enthusiasm as he patted Reese on the back. "I'd better go find Isabella. I left her with a group from the Italian consulate." Turning to go, he checked his step. "Friends?" He offered his hand.

Reese took it. "Friends."

As Reese watched Duncan cross the dance floor, his own words echoed in his mind: *"I'm sure Beth will tell me when she's ready."* And she would be as soon as he assured her that their relationship meant more to him than a casual season fling. Once he asked her to move in with him things would start to change.

He shoved a nervous set of fingers through his hair as he thought about the magnitude of Beth Langdon's presence in his life. Their relationship had started out like a refreshing breath of spring air, but had quickly turned into something as necessary as an oasis in the middle of a desert. He was coming to depend on her for everything real, right and worthwhile. When they were apart he went through the motions of living his everyday life, while he counted the hours until they would be together again. He once couldn't wait for the sun to go down, he now couldn't wait for it to rise, because that meant a new day had begun. A day he might spend with Beth. His whole life was slowly and steadily reconfiguring around a new center. And it was time to let her know that she was that center.

"Teddy Bear? It's Beth. Guess who I was dancing with tonight?" She looked across the bedroom at

Reese, who had removed his jacket and unknotted his tie, leaving the lengths of black silk to rest on either side of his collar. "Yes, I mean besides my Frenchman," she said, taking in his mischievous grin as he undid his shirt. The starched, pleated shirtfront fell open, revealing a mat of dark, curly chest hair. She tried not to stare at the healthy signs of masculinity, but it was impossible. She'd seen him in street clothes, in swim trunks and dressed to perfection in his formal wear, but this image of casual abandon pulled at every fiber of her feminine being. He'd been making bedroom eyes at her all evening, and knowing him so intimately, she quickly turned away before he did something else to make her gasp.

"Okay, okay, I'll tell you," she said as she saw Reese's shirt flying by her. "Your favorite member of European royalty. Yes! Really, Teddy! I'm not kidding."

Even through her sister's scream of delight and hurried questions, she heard the distinct sound of Reese unzipping his trousers. "Well, he's taller than you think," she said, sneaking a peek at Reese. "Reese, how tall would you say the prince is?"

Standing several feet away from her, he tilted his head and demonstrated another scandalously long body measurement with his hands. Shaking a shame-on-you hand at his audacious behavior, she walked toward the mirror while she tried stifling a giggle. "Oh, he's a big guy, Teddy. Listen, I just had to let you know I met him and that he was absolutely charming." She paused when a condom packet landed on the floor next to her. "Yes, Teddy, as in Prince Charming. I've got to go," she said when Reese stepped behind her, wrapped his arms around her waist and pulled her back against him. "I've got some pressing business I've got to get to. I'll call you tomorrow when I can talk longer. I love you, too," she said, clicking off the phone and dropping it onto an armchair.

When Reese stepped to the side to string kisses along her neck she pulled in a startled breath. With his bare hip and leg reflecting in the mirror, she realized he'd stripped off the rest of his clothes. That he was naked while she was fully clothed provided her with a strange surge of feminine power. A rush of heat seemed to liquefy that power and plunged her helplessly into a simmering pool of desire. Reaching back, she ran her hand over his muscular hip and hair-roughened thigh. "I can't pretend with you." Leaning her head to one side, she accepted his kisses and encouraged more with the restless weaving of her shoulders.

"Can't pretend about what?"

She met his reflected gaze in the mirror. "You make me want you so much I can't catch my breath."

Whispering in French, he unzipped her gown and began lowering it. Together they watched in the mirror as each creamy white inch of her was slowly revealed above the taffeta roses. After settling the gown at her waist, he drew his hands up her rib cage until he was caressing her breasts. Circling their tips with light strokes from his fingers and thumbs, he whispered hotly against her cheek, "*Mon ange polisson,* you're too beautiful. Look, you're like a sin waiting to happen."

Stepping closer, he crossed his arms over her body and gently finessed her nipples to tingling points of pleasure. Moving her hips provocatively against him, she felt the gown sliding lower.

"Like sin," he whispered again, running his hands down the front of her body to slide the fabric below her navel.

He pressed his hips forward and the evidence of his need throbbed hot and hard against her spine. The sight of their mirrored lovemaking sent an intensified rush of pleasure to the slick heat between her thighs. She couldn't imagine performing this erotic taboo with anyone else but Reese. A moan broke in her throat as she reached back for him again.

"Why do you make that sound?" he asked, staring in the mirror as his one hand wandered past her navel and under the white taffeta chastely draping the bottom half of her.

"When I'm with you, like this, you make me feel so safe...so sinfully safe that I think I'd do anything you asked."

"Beth," he whispered again and again, as he stroked the pearls at her neck with one hand while he palmed the damp material between her thighs with the other. "I only ask that you trust me."

When his feathery touches brought her near the edge of ecstasy, she pulled his hand away. "One sin for you," she whispered, moving forward and shimmying out of her gown. She quickly stripped off her thigh-high stockings and panties. Turning to him, she stepped out of the mound of silk and taffeta, then kicked it aside. She knelt in front of him, drawing her fingers down his thighs as she went. Taking him in both of her hands, she brought her lips close to him. "And one for me."

She heard him curse, first in words she could understand and then in words she could only guess at. She continued the intimate act until he reached down to her shoulders and begged her to stop. When she released him, he knelt beside her, then gently tumbled her to the rug. He managed a short, breathless smile as he reached for the condom packet and tore it open.

"Have you had enough sin yet?" he asked as he readied himself.

"Not nearly," she said, as a sense of urgency overtook her. Planting a foot on the floor, she reached for him, but he was already levering himself between her parting thighs. Lifting her hips to meet his thrust, she took him in with a breaking cry. The moment for coherent sentences had passed, and now all they could manage were whispered words and breathless gasps.

"There..."

"Trust me...right there..."

"Yes...yes..."

"More?"

"Yes...don't stop..."

"Hold me...now."

"Now!"

At the moment of their shared surrender, the world shuddered away leaving them to soar through the richest pleasure they'd ever known. Long after the sweet, fierce pulsations stopped echoing through their joined flesh, Reese continued to hold her. As he stroked her cheek in the breathless afterglow, she drew lazy circles in the hair around one of his nipples. He took a deep breath. If now wasn't the right time to bring up the subject, there would never be a right time. "We need to talk about something."

Beth's fingers suddenly stilled. Warning prickles zipped up her spine. "What's that?"

"I want you to think about moving in with me." He shifted her in his arms to look down at her face. "I don't have to tell you how pleasant it would be."

Why hadn't she seen this coming? And what would moving in with him accomplish except to drive her mad with guilt every waking second. "I...well, yes. But I promised Billy I'd stay at his place until he got back. You know, he's going to have the final word on whether or not to open a gallery here in Europe. He expects me...I mean, somehow it doesn't seem right to take off and—"

"Beth, Waleska won't care. I hear he's still in Fiji with his friends."

"We were close..." she began as she pulled away and sat up. The lies kept growing and so did her feeling of panic. "He's—"

Pushing himself up, Reese leaned against the wall. "Close? Are you trying to make me jealous?" he asked, arching one brow.

"What's so funny?"

"You are. Beth, Billy Waleska was never your lover."

"How can you say that? You don't know—"

"Billy Waleska is gay. Openly and happily gay." When she didn't respond, Reese's good-natured smile disappeared to a blank stare. "If you'd ever met him you would know that."

Eight

"Beth, this is Reese talking to you. Reese, the man who knows more intimate secrets about you than your sister, your hairdresser and your gynecologist combined. You have to realize that you can trust me by now. I'd never betray you. I swear, whatever it is, I'll understand."

Turning away from him, she pulled her legs up to her chest and wrapped her arms around them. Her blatantly protective move was no deterrent to him.

Pressing his palms to the carpet, he leaned in inches from her. "Listen to me, what we have is too important not to pursue. We need to see where this is going. You know that." He plowed his fingers through his hair, then closed his hand over her arms. "God, Beth, say you know that."

Reese's stare penetrated to the center of her soul. If only for partial relief from the guilt clawing at her insides, she had to give him something. "You're right. Billy was never my lover. I've never even met him."

He nodded slowly. "What else?"

"I—I don't own a chain of decorating galleries."

"Is someone following you? Is that why you left the States? To escape your past and reinvent yourself?" He asked his questions gently, carefully, giving her space and time to answer. But all he was doing was skewering her through the heart with his pointed concern.

She bit down on her lip to keep from blurting out the truth. Every word of it. But she hadn't lost her mind yet. Confessing everything at this point might clear her conscience. But that would bring only momentary relief. "I know you want more answers, but I can't give them to you. Not now."

After a moment Reese took his hand away and eased back against the wall. "When?"

Lifting her arms, she dropped them in a sign of helplessness. Her chin quivered. "I don't know."

"It's okay. I'm not going to force you to tell."

She stared at him as tears pricked at her eyes. If he was any more gentle and understanding, she would have to scream. He hadn't taken his eyes from her since he'd asked about Billy. "Do you want me to go?" she asked, knowing that was the last thing he wanted and the last thing she could afford to do.

"Beth?" he said, looking as if she'd asked him to do something bizarre, something unthinkable. "I want you to let me help you."

"I don't know if you'll ever be able to do that," she said over the insistent voice inside her head. *Why prolong this agony any longer? Lay it all on the line, then ask him to deny that he's Harrison Montgomery's son.*

The rational part of her mind wasn't ready to risk the project and the part ruled by her heart wasn't brave enough to give him up. Moving in with him was the only choice. Then, while Reese thought she was coming closer to revealing her past, he would be coming closer to her. Close enough, she hoped, that he would admit to her of his own accord that he was Harrison Montgomery's bastard son. And then what?

"Beth, listen to me. I want you out of Waleska's place and over here with me," he said, his quiet, take-charge tone commanding her to listen. "We'll go away for a few weeks. And when I can prove to you that you can trust me, you're going to tell me all of it. I swear, we'll figure something out."

She smoothed her fingers over a tear-coated cheek as she tried to stop her quivering chin. She didn't want to think about Montgomery anymore. She wanted to feel safe and sheltered and free from guilt. And more than anything she wanted to be with Reese. "Wh-where would we go? Up to the olive-mill house?" They'd already spent a few nights there overseeing the electrician's work and directing the delivery and placement of new furniture. She was almost relieved when he shook his head. The country house held too many memories already. Spending what she knew would be their last days together there would be bittersweet poison.

"We'll go up to Château Beaumont."

"Are you sure you want to do that?" she asked, alarmed that she would have to meet his mother, Sylvie Beaumont Marchand. The mother of Harrison Montgomery's son.

"My family's expecting me anyway. Don't look so frightened. They will welcome you."

Beth pressed her hands against her mouth as hot tears spilled down her cheeks. Whoever said that love made you stronger was wrong. Her love for Reese was killing her. How in the name of all that was good and right would she be able to look those people in the eye knowing she was betraying their son, their brother? She looked up at Reese. She rubbed her temples as specks of black stars buzzed in front of her eyes.

"Beth, are you okay?"

Her words choked in her throat and she had to try a second time to speak. "I'm fine. I'm just thinking about what I have to do to move out of Billy's tomorrow."

As he reached for her with his outstretched arms, Reese heaved a sigh of relief that made her tears flow harder. She burrowed deeper into his embrace and for a few precious heartbeats the rest of the world stayed outside the strong circle of his arms.

"I'll drive you over to Cap Ferrat tomorrow so you can get your things. We could leave for the château from there, but I've got to finish up some work at my office."

His sense of immediacy was beginning to rub off on her. She suddenly felt as if she had to hurry, too, even though she knew she was rushing headlong toward the inevitable moment of reckoning. But the sooner she went away with him the more time she would have with him before the world fell apart.

She brushed away her tears. "I've got a better idea. I'll drop you at your office and go over myself. The maid can help me and this way you'll have all morning to do what you have to there."

He frowned. "You'll be all right going alone?" he asked, his reluctant tone touching her deeply.

"Of course I will," she said, rubbing his cheekbone with her thumb. "Why would you worry about that?"

"I have this crazy feeling that if I let you out of my sight, you'll disappear."

"I'll be back here before noon tomorrow and settled in by the time you come home."

"We'll celebrate then," he said, his furrowed brow smoothing at last. "Where would you like to go? Café de Paris?"

She shook her head.

"Where?" he asked, looking at her as if he were seeing something wonderful and infinitely interesting for the first time. "I'll take you any place you want."

"How about that restaurant where they play Buddy Holly on the jukebox and—"

"Serve the best cheeseburgers on the Riviera? Excellent choice," he said, kissing her shoulders.

Smiling, she ruffled his hair as an unexpected ripple of hope passed through her. As incredible as the thought was, she had to wonder if miracles happened anymore. If the pain of the past weeks would disappear, leaving only the pleasure and the promise of loving Reese Marchand.

Next morning as she parked the Jaguar under the villa's portico, Beth attempted to push away the fantasy that she'd entertained last night. Stepping out of the car, she gave the door a solid slam. She had no business imagining a future with Reese. None at all. But still the images tumbled in. Every sweet, sexy, domestic scenario of conjugal bliss possible.

Her heart was already tripping double time as she headed past the colonnade and into the house. As wild and improbable as she knew it to be, her head and heart were suddenly filled with hope again. She was in love with Reese, and even though Reese hadn't said the words, he was in love with her. And wasn't there always hope where there was love? Was she crazy to even think that Reese could hear the whole story, then offer to help? Being raised in luxury and afforded every advantage didn't mean a person was blind to those not so fortunate. Just last night hadn't he proven what a decent, caring, loving man he was? Hurrying down the hall, she pushed open the door and went in. The birds were chirping in the trees outside, the sun was pouring in through the open door to the terrace and the scents of citrus and roses were wafting through the room. Blame it on an adrenaline high, she told herself, but absolutely anything seemed possible.

Taking her suitcase from the dressing room, she brought it to the bed and opened it there. She'd planned to leave most of her wardrobe behind, but there were a few items she couldn't do without. Reaching into her lingerie drawer, she pulled out several pastel teddies. As she hurried back to the suitcase one of them dropped from her grasp and she reached to pick it up.

The voice came out of nowhere, calm and deceptively friendly. "Going somewhere?"

The rest of the lingerie spilled from her hands as she whirled around toward the hall door. "Eugene. I...yes," she managed to say over her heart, now lodged in her throat. "Reese wants me to move in with him."

"My, my," he said, tapping his fingers on a manila envelope he held. Stepping into the room, he picked up a handful of lilac satin from the rug. Rubbing the lace-edged teddy, he passed it under his nostrils before placing it in her outstretched hand. "You've been a busy girl, Beth."

"I'm just doing my job," she said, disgusted by what he'd just done. She held back admonishing him for his crudeness. As objectionable as Eugene could be, his action was over the top even for him. Instinct told her that something was terribly wrong and the smartest move for her was to remain calm. "What are you doing here?" she asked, tossing the lingerie into her suitcase.

"I get a little edgy when people don't return my calls. It's been over three weeks. How long did you think I'd wait?"

"I told you. You have to be patient."

"I was patient…for three weeks. Now I'm going to do something else."

"What?" she asked, feeling suddenly queasy.

"I'm going to get myself introduced to a certain Mr. Marchand and then he and I are going to have a little talk."

She felt the blood draining from her head. "Why would you do that?"

"Your dawdling has left me no choice."

"I'm doing the best I can."

"Not good enough. The campaign is in bad shape, and as President Pierson's special assistant, I've run out of issues that I believe could be helpful in getting him reelected."

"Issues? Don't you mean—"

"Call it whatever you like," he said, cutting her off. "After your friend's lead on that cowboy Lucas Caldwell petered out, I thought I had two more shots at bringing down Montgomery's campaign. Unfortunately the other lead ended in a weed-choked graveyard in Mississippi." He shook his head. "I thought we'd stumbled on Montgomery's mother lode of indiscretions a few months ago, but it's all come down to one. And I'm going to make this one count." He locked gazes with Beth. "You, me and Marchand have a lot of work to do."

Her skin felt as if it were simultaneously burning and freezing. The quiet desperation in Eugene's voice frightened her. Moving away from him, she sat down on the bed. "I don't get it."

"Sure you do. I need to convince Reese Marchand to release a statement to the press—"

She came off the bed as if it were covered in red-hot coals. "You never said anything about getting *him* to make a public announcement."

"I'm saying it now, so sit down and listen." She eased back on the bed. "That's better. Serious times call for serious actions, Beth. Because of my close position to the president, I would rather not risk getting my own hands dirty. But since you're apparently incapable of getting the job done, you're forcing me to."

"All right!" she said, wiping her face with a cold hand. "You made your point. I promise you, I'll talk to him this weekend."

Eugene opened the manila envelope. "You'd better do a good job of convincing him, Beth. But in case he refuses to cooperate or if he denies that Montgomery's his father, I have these to use with the story." He withdrew several eight-by-ten photos and dropped them into her lap.

She recognized them immediately. They were of her and Reese taken the day he'd surprised her at the outdoor café, almost a month ago. Her heart sank to her stomach. All along they'd thought the paparazzi had been taking photos of the prince and his girlfriend. Looking through the pictures, she remembered the delight she'd experienced when Reese had pulled the scarf from his pocket. When he'd wrapped it around her neck. When he'd kissed her. A wave of nausea hit her and she licked at her dry lips. "They're very good."

"Good? Hell, they're great. Almost too high quality for something like the *American Investigator.*"

"You'd release these to a tabloid?"

"What are you worried about? No one would recognize you with all that hair blocking your profile. But they sure as hell will recognize Marchand's resemblance to Montgomery." He shrugged. "If we don't get Marchand's cooperation, we'll have to take the low road. Any reputable newspaper wouldn't touch this story without some kind of verification." He smiled and shook his head. "It's a shame to waste these on Willis Herkner, but I know he'd love having these to run beside his articles."

Reese's words were playing again in her mind: *"Beth, having your privacy invaded in such a dishonest, such a sleazy way is unforgivable."* She fanned herself with the photos.

"Hey, are you okay? You look like you're about to pass out."

"Too many late nights," she said, working at doing the best lying she'd ever done in her life and holding herself together while she did it. Tossing the photos on her bed as if they were disposable moments in her life and not pieces ripped from her heart, she smiled at Eugene. "Those won't be necessary. He's taking me to his mother's tomorrow. I'll ask him there."

He studied her coldly before a tight, thin-lipped smile moved half his face. "See that you do. In the meantime," he said, opening the door and stepping out on the terrace, "I'll lay low here and wait. I don't want the press getting wind that I'm over here." He withdrew a cigarette from a silver case, lit it and inhaled deeply. "Nice life if you have time for it," he said, waving the cigarette toward the perfectly kept grounds and the topiary hedges. "Waleska knows how to live." He shook his head, then leaned back against the door.

"You didn't tell me he was gay."

Eugene laughed softly as he loosened his tie. "I don't tell you a lot of things," he said, before the faraway look in his eyes began to focus on her again. He moved away from the door, his manner and mood changing as he pointed a finger at her. His voice was suddenly brusque and his words to the point. "Listen, I want you back here with Marchand by the middle of the week. Don't give me that look. You've had all summer to get cozy with him. The payoff has to be now."

The magnitude of what she'd been doing, of the lies she continued to tell and the half-truths she had to tiptoe around suddenly hit her. As she'd known it would someday. The world had come to an abrupt and jarring stop and it was time to get off.

"You look green."

"Oh, God, I think I'm going to be sick," she said, hurrying into the bathroom and slamming the door shut.

Nine

Beth watched the litter of King Charles spaniels nipping at Reese's hair while his six-year-old twin nephews, holding him to the ground, pummeled him with their fists. His exaggerated growls and dramatic gestures sent the boys into fits of laughter. The idyllic scene could have been taking place on any lawn in America, but it was taking place in the back garden of Château Beaumont. Beth looked up at the turrets of the centuries-old structure and marveled at the abilities of the woman beside her. The happy and loving Sylvie Marchand and her family filled the great house with warmth and laughter.

Sylvie slipped her hands around Beth's arm. "My son is going to make a wonderful father someday."

"I have no doubt that he will," Beth said, hoping her cheerful reply would mask the turmoil inside her. She would be worlds away when that blessing was bestowed on Reese. *And one day when his sons are old enough, he will warn them about women like me.*

Looking back at Reese, she saw him disengage himself from his nephews and the puppies. Sylvie leaned her head close to Beth's, and in a conspiratorial voice, she whispered, "And I think the olive-mill house would be a delightful place to raise his children. Don't you agree?"

Unable to meet Reese's mother's gaze, Beth nodded as she pictured Reese with his own sons. As he made his way to the terrace, the lump in her throat grew bigger, threatening to choke her. This was slow suicide. "Delightful," she said to Sylvie as he climbed the broad step.

"What are you two whispering about?" he asked, leaning to kiss them both.

"Beth and I were talking about what is still needed to make your house a proper home," Sylvie said as he poured himself a tumbler of iced tea. She turned to Beth. "Philippe and I have so many lovely things here at the château. Perhaps it is time to, how do you say, circulate a few of them within the family?"

Before Beth could respond, Reese raised the glass to his mother, his smile both teasing and affectionate. "Mother has always believed that it's preferable to bring something down from your grandfather's attic rather than to buy it new."

"But, Reese," Sylvie said, a mild reprimand apparent in her tone, "I wouldn't insist you take anything. I want Beth to use only what she feels would work well with the rest of her choices." She reached for Beth's hand, then patted it. "And what I want to offer today is not something from my dusty attic but something from my sitting room. Would you be interested in having a look at it?''

''Yes, of course,'' she said, slipping her hand from Sylvie's. *I will agree to anything as long as you'll stop treating me so kindly.* Reaching down, she picked up one of the puppies that had wandered onto the terrace, closed her eyes and exhaled into its fur. Two full days of experiencing Sylvie's charm and grace—where was the broken, bitter woman she'd expected? This was worse than a forced meeting between Mata Hari and Mother Teresa.

''What did you have in mind, Mother?'' Reese asked, as he reached to tug on the whiskers of the puppy Beth was holding. The sandy-haired twins rushed onto the terrace at that moment and, whooping loudly, began running circles around them.

''The tapestry across from the fireplace. You know, the one with the pheasants and flowers and woodland scene. Why don't you take Beth in there and show it to her?'' she said, picking up the other puppies and putting them into a large basket. Taking her grandsons' hands, she looked up at her son. ''I'll take these two little warriors to the vineyard so we can tell their grandfather that lunch will be ready in an hour.''

Reese and his mother slipped into speaking French and Beth settled the last puppy into the basket. As she started to stand up, both twins let go of their grandmother, wound their arms around Beth's neck and kissed her. The spontaneous acts of affection brought her to her knees. While she was returning their kisses, she was aware that both Sylvie and Reese had barely noticed. *And why should they?* she asked herself. *Genuine affection flowed easily through the Mar-*

chand family. Beth let go of the boys and stood up, re-
alizing she couldn't put off the inevitable any longer.

Since the first moment she'd seen Reese, she knew
what had to be done. There was never going to be a
right moment to confront him, and to endure any more
of his family's kindnesses would surely drive her mad.
This guilt eating at her was only complicating the situation by scattering her focus. She had to stop thinking about the Marchands, too. They were a strong and
united family, more than capable of taking care of
themselves during a crisis. What she had to focus her
concern on were the have-nots. Those families who
deserved roofs over their heads as much as the Marchands.

When Sylvie started off the terrace, Beth impul-
sively took her hand. "Wait. Please."

"Yes?" Sylvie asked, her eyes warm and attentive.

"I wanted to tell you how much I appreciate you and
your husband's hospitality," she said, surprised at how
calm her voice sounded. "I know you weren't expecting me, but you've never given me a hint that I was
unwelcome. Thank you. It means more to me than
you'll ever know." Letting go of Sylvie's hand, she
wrapped her arms tightly around her own middle.
"That's all I wanted to say," she said, finally managing to swallow part of the lump in her throat.

What had possessed her to reach out that way? Once
the Marchands found out how she'd planned to betray
them all along, this pathetic show of gratitude would
be seen for what it was. A desperate attempt to prove
she wasn't totally ruthless.

Sylvie's gentle gaze drifted toward her son, then back
to Beth. "Even if you weren't the cause for my son's
happiness, it's wonderful having you here." In more of

a loving act than a momentary impulse, Sylvie drew her into her arms. "I know how much you love him, my dear," she whispered, then walked out onto the lawn with her grandsons.

Love him? Yes, Beth wanted to say. *With all my heart. But now I'm going to hurt him. Maybe even destroy him. And you, too. I have no choice now, Sylvie. And for what it's worth, I don't think I ever did.*

If Reese hadn't taken her by the hand and headed toward Sylvie's private sitting room, Beth didn't know how long she would have stood there watching her. The mother of the man she loved. The mother of Harrison Montgomery's son.

Reese glanced at Beth as he led her down the west hallway and opened a door. "We used to call this Mother's retreat." He waited for her to smile, and when she didn't the uneasiness in his eyes didn't escape her. He continued on as if the word *suspicion* wasn't in his vocabulary. "Ever since Mother mentioned the tapestry I've been picturing it," he said, as he walked over to the heavy rectangle of cloth on the wall, "hanging against the stones at the bottom of the stairs." He raised his brows but continued. "Mother says she acquired it before she married. I don't know much about its history except that it was bought at an auction in Paris," he said, as he began running his hand over the finely woven work of art. Stopping his hand halfway, he turned to make a humorous face. "I can tell by all that enthusiasm that you're not sure about it, are you?"

"Reese, I don't want to talk about the tapestry. I want to talk about something important. I can't put this off any longer."

He drew in a deep breath as his smile slipped from his face. "Yes, of course. Take your time." He reached for a chair. "Maybe you had better sit down."

"Maybe *you* had better sit down," she said, pacing away from him.

"It's okay," he said, "you know you can tell me anything."

She meant to ease into it, but because he was being so understanding, she knew she had to get on with her task. Even so, as she turned to face him the words rushed out of her faster than she wanted them to. "I work for the committee to reelect President Pierson. I was asked to come over here and find out the truth."

Reese closed his hands over the back of the chair. He would swear he was hearing what sounded like a revolver being cocked as another piece of the puzzle that was Beth Langdon clicked into place. She kept her gaze flickering to and from his until he spoke. "And what truth would that be?"

"That you're Harrison Montgomery's son."

If she'd pointed that revolver at him and pulled the trigger, Reese wouldn't have felt a thing. His brain was too busy exploding with a hundred different thoughts. All of them incredulous. All of them painful. And all he could do was laugh. A dry crack of a laugh that belied the cold shock descending over him. Still, he had to try one more time to make it go away. "Didn't we have a go-round before about this?"

She held her silence and her breath.

A macabre joke suddenly careered into his mind. Maybe she *had* shot him and he hadn't realized it until now. And while the part of him that she'd played for a fool lay bleeding on the floor, the older, wiser part began to gather strength. The part that he had been showing to the world for over a quarter of a century. The part that knew all about surviving and not feeling. He slipped a hand in his pocket and snorted with self-disgust. He should have seen this coming. The signs were all there. Her acute interest in anything to do with the election. Her clever evasions that she inevitably rounded back on him as a question. Her uncanny timing every step of the way. And so much more. "I see. If you can simply verify your claim, President Pierson can point America's morality radar at Montgomery and I'll show up as the blip on the screen. The product of a reckless indiscretion during his salad days, his unclaimed love child, whose existence proves he's unfit for the presidency." Reese pulled a blade of grass from his shirt sleeve and flicked it away. "Just tell me one thing, Beth. Did they tell you to lie back and think of your country? Or was that your idea?"

Beth forced herself to reach beyond the sting of his words. "I know I deserve that and worse for what I did to you, but there's a reason why I went to these extraordinary lengths—"

"Sex and politics?" he asked. "I fail to see why you'd think that combination is so extraordinary."

"Reese, I never thought things would go the way they did with us. I can't begin to tell you…I don't have the words to say how sorry I am," she said, pressing her hands to her middle.

"Sorry? I would think you'd be quite proud of yourself." He closed his eyes for a second as he ran his fingers through his hair. "Before I met you, I prided myself on my cynicism. But you managed to change that in a matter of minutes. You waltzed in, dressed in your oh-so-pure white gown, looking like an angel, and threw yourself right into the center of my life. Oh, and that little thing you managed with the pearls?'' He shook his head, more at himself than at her. "You were really very good."

"Reese, please listen to me. Sometimes it's necessary to put personal...matters aside, to try to forget our own situations for the sake of a greater good," she said, her words sounding hollow even to herself. When he gave her a disbelieving look, she lifted her fists and splayed her fingers. "Don't you see? I couldn't live with myself if I didn't do what I could for a cause I believe in." For one crazy moment she thought she saw his eyes narrow as he considered what she said. In the next second he shook his head again, slowly this time.

"God save us all from true believers."

"Damn you and your perfect life," she shouted, slamming her hands on the writing desk next to them. "Look at yourself. Look at this house. This life you're swaggering through—"

Taking her by the elbows, he pulled her hard against him. "Does all that make it my fault that middle-class America isn't good enough for you? What are you really after here? To land yourself some cushy job at the White House? Is that it? A little glitz and glamour Washington style at the expense of me and my family?" He shook her. "My God, don't you know what this is about?"

"Yes. If you'll let me explain—"

"No. It's my turn to talk. Harrison Montgomery may or may not have a secret to hide, but if you want a full-blown study on moral corruption take a hard look at Pierson. At what he's done. At what he's asked you to do."

"But you don't know the whole truth—"

"Beth, you've told me so many lies, I wouldn't recognize the truth if it accidentally slipped out of that talented mouth of yours."

"No. Please, don't say that."

"Look what they got you to do. Sleep with a man you didn't love. A man who never asked or expected anything but honesty. A man who went so far as to accept you into his life, invite you into his family's home. And now you're begging him to be nice?"

"You've got me all wrong."

"Why should it matter to you if I've got you all wrong? You had *me* nailed. Isn't that the important thing?"

"What do you mean?" she asked, feeling the blood draining from her face.

"If you'd asked me sooner maybe we wouldn't have had to go through all this."

"Reese—"

"Do I have to say it, Beth?" he asked, drawing her closer. "Do you need to hear me say the words to make it official? Okay. Harrison Montgomery is my father." He stared hard into her eyes.

"But why wouldn't you want him to tell the world that fact?"

"I never cared if he told the world—I just wanted him to tell me."

Beth held her breath, then closed her eyes and let it out in a trembling exhalation. The numbing moment held no victory. Devoid of any emotion she could recognize, she vaguely wondered when her hands would stop shaking and her legs would stop feeling like rubber. When he let go, she opened her eyes and grabbed on to the edge of the desk. Forcing herself to remain standing, she watched him head for the door.

Breathing was an effort and, because of the black spots flitting in front of her eyes, so was seeing. Even if she could make herself speak, this wasn't the time to call him back. She pressed her hand to her stomach. As miserable as moments in her childhood had been, both of her parents were always there for her. Accepting. Supporting. Loving. But for all of Reese Marchand's blessings, he'd suffered a deprivation she could only imagine. Rejection and denial by his own flesh and blood. He'd been haunted by that unfinished business all of his life. And she'd been the instrument to tear away the scab, probe into the depths of his wounded soul and start him bleeding again. Nothing Beth had ever imagined had prepared her for the anguish and guilt she felt for Reese.

Reaching for the chair, she sat down heavily and waited for the worst to pass. Rational thoughts. That's what she had to hold on to now, she told herself. She looked at her hands again, turning them palm down before running them over her thighs. That was strange. She could barely feel her own touch. And for one hysterical moment she wondered if she'd ever feel anything again.

In a few seconds the surreal moment stopped, leaving her alone with the hard reality of what she'd done. She glanced up at the tapestry, and their time together at the olive-mill house came rushing back to her. Every laughing, joyful, tender and intimate moment they'd shared danced around her like hell's avenging angels. She stood up and moved toward the door to escape their taunting images. If she didn't get out of this house, she was going to start screaming and never stop. Fumbling for the brass lever, she yanked the door open, then froze on the threshold.

Sylvie studied her for long moment. "Reese told me just now in the hallway," she said quietly as she stepped into the room and eased the door closed. "Telling him all of that must have been painful for you."

"Yes," she said, desperate that Sylvie should know that fact, as incongruous as it sounded at the moment. "Telling him was the most painful thing I've ever had to do." Staggered by Sylvie's compassionate manner, Beth wondered how much Reese left out when he'd told his mother. "Maybe Reese didn't tell you all of it."

"I believe he told me everything," she said, gently closing her hands around Beth's elbows. "But as you can imagine, he was in no mood to pick and choose his words."

Beth looked down at Sylvie's hands as the older woman stroked her arms. "Then why are you being so kind to me now that you know the truth?"

"Because I love him, too, and because I knew one day something such as this had to happen."

Easing away from Sylvie, she rubbed at her forehead as she tried to make sense of the moment. "Sylvie, I've betrayed your son's trust in order to ensure that Harrison Montgomery won't win the election. Why aren't you dragging me out of your home by my hair? Why aren't you throwing stones at me? Or cursing me into an even darker corner of hell than I'm already in?"

"My dear, what a time you have had," she said, smoothing back a lock of Beth's hair.

"Both of you have no idea why this is so important to me."

"I do not doubt that you have good reason. And when the smoke clears from around my beloved son's stubborn head, he will want you to explain. But right now we have something more important to talk about."

"More important?" she asked, boggled by where Sylvie could be taking this.

"Reese's father. Whether you have little regard for him or think that he is a monster, I want you to know that the Monty I knew was quite human."

Beth shook her head. "Sylvie, the man is not who he says he is. He's lying to get what he wants."

"From time to time, aren't we all guilty of that?"

The indirect reference to Beth's situation caused her to step back. "But if it's for a good...cause..." Her words drifted away, leaving her to brace herself against a disturbing wave of uncertainty. "Go on," she said, forcing the thought to the back of her mind.

"I was nineteen and going to school in Paris at the time. And Monty was a young and handsome bachelor diplomat with a reputation for a roving eye...until he met me." She shook her head. "From the first moment we knew how it would be. He was so brash, so American, insisting he wanted to experience the real France, something beyond the rigid protocol of his embassy position." Giving an exaggerated shrug, she laughed like a schoolgirl about to share a secret. "So what could I do but play him my Edith Piaf records, take him to Brigitte Bardot movies and teach him to eat snails? I believe those months that we were lovers were the happiest of his life. Away from his family, and from the political machine that was already grooming him for this campaign, he was allowed to live without the burden of his—what did he end up calling it?—destiny." Sylvie walked to the window and pulled aside the curtain. "But lovers hold folly as dear as good sense, and one night out there on the riverbank we gave in to our passion. We were careful only with the pleasure we gave each other.''

While Sylvie paused to remember her private moment, Beth recalled the first afternoon at the olive-mill house when she and Reese had taken a similar chance. Before she could allow herself to consider the logical implications of that impetuous moment, Sylvie went on.

"Those nasty river swans . . . we tried to ignore their protests. We wanted to enjoy the moonlight, too. And we did," she said, finally giving in to laughter. "But only after Monty left my arms to shoo them away."

Beth steeled herself against laughing with her. As romantic as Sylvie's recollections sounded, she wasn't going to be that easily swayed into believing that Harrison Montgomery was a good guy. "Sylvie, Montgomery left you pregnant and unmarried. If he was that selfish, that irresponsible with you, why should he be trusted to act responsibly as a president?''

Sighing, Sylvie crossed the room to the writing desk. Opening a hidden compartment, she drew out an envelope. "I would be lying if I told you I wasn't devastated for a while after he went back. But while he chose to pursue what he believed was his destiny, I had our beautiful baby, and I will always be grateful to Monty for him." She clasped the envelope to her breast as her face rounded into a smile. "Oh, Beth, what a beautiful baby Reese was. I would sit here in this room for hours, kissing his fingers and toes, listening to his laughter, loving him. And with Philippe in my life, God soon blessed me again with our three daughters."

Beth swallowed hard as Sylvie placed the envelope in her hands. She could only imagine the depth of emotions this woman had faced in her lifetime. While she had been instantly impressed when she met Sylvie, she now had a deep respect for her.

"Reese has never seen this, but I want you to read it...to know his father better. If after reading it you still want to go through with your plans, that is up to you."

Sitting down, Beth ran her fingertips over the strong, masculine scrawl on the envelope that read simply "Sylvie." She slid out the letter, then raised her gaze again. "Are you sure you want to share this with me?" When the older woman nodded, then moved back to the window, Beth unfolded the letter and began to read.

My dearest Sylvie,
These are the hardest words I've ever had to write. I have made the decision to go back to America. Too many people have been counting on this course for me all of my life and so have I. Believe me when I tell you that I love you now and I'll love you always. If there were any way I could marry you and raise this child of mine that you carry, then I would do it. Since my father and his men arrived, I've thought of nothing else but finding that way. I even considered sending for you in a few months, but I couldn't shame you further by keeping you hidden away as my mistress.

Sylvie, darling, how could a time so precious to me and, I know, to you, too, come apart in a few short weeks? I will have doubts about my decision to leave you and our baby for the rest of my days, but something is pulling me and I can't pretend it's not. Is it destiny? I don't know. Maybe I never will for sure.

There will always be questions in my mind and in my heart, but we have to go our separate ways now. Please give our child all the love I can't give him and know that I will think of him and the precious memories I share with his mother often. Because we must both make new lives for ourselves, I want you to know that I won't interfere with yours or with our child's.

I'm leaving my heart with you, Sylvie. I won't have any use for it now, because it's broken in pieces. Forgive me.

Monty

Beth folded the letter and replaced it in the envelope, knowing she couldn't bear to read it again. The genuine emotions inspiring the letter were undeniable. Harrison Montgomery had loved Sylvie, but still he had chosen to walk away. The man had given up the love of a remarkable and unforgettable woman and eventually had made a politically correct marriage for himself. A marriage that provided him with a broader constituency, but no more children. Whatever regrets, whatever misgivings he'd experienced because of that decision thirty-five years ago had to still haunt him.

"Did you ever see him again?" she asked, taking the letter to Sylvie and placing it in her hand.

"At the time he wrote the letter my parents were so terribly upset. I was barely twenty years old. They along with Monty's father wouldn't let us near each other." She smiled and for a few seconds her eyes took on that faraway look again. "We managed to spend one more night together, crying in each other's arms," she said, turning toward the window. For a long time neither of them spoke. "So you see, Harrison Montgomery isn't such a monster, is he?"

"No," Beth said as a partial weight lifted from her shoulders. After reading his letter, Harrison Montgomery had become for her exactly what Sylvie had said he would. Human. Filled with misgivings, struggling to do the right thing and needing to love and be loved in the process. Whether she agreed with his politics or not, he was as subject to the world he lived in as anyone else. "Harrison Montgomery was a man who had a difficult decision to make. With either choice he must have known he would be giving up something he would never have again."

"You understand perfectly. But time is a great healer for most of us. It appears things have worked out for Monty. He's at last come to his moment." She drew a fingertip beneath her eye as she crossed the room to the desk. "His decision eventually worked out for everyone except our son."

"What do you mean?" she asked as Sylvie put the letter away. "What hasn't worked out for Reese?"

"He was nine years old when I told him about his father. He asked the questions I knew he would, and I answered him as truthfully and as gently as I could for such a little boy. But I came to realize that my explanations weren't enough and over the years his childish fascination with this man he's never known has grown into an obsession."

Beth thought back over the summer, remembering the times Reese had spoken out about Montgomery. While she had railed on against him, Reese had managed to turn around many of her arguments. And he only could have accomplished that by a meticulous knowledge of Montgomery. The kind of knowledge

that came from careful and dedicated study. Reese was
holding on to a fragile hope, a lifelong dream to know
and understand his father. Staggered by her sudden
awareness of that truth, she pressed her hands to her
face. "Sylvie, what have I done to him?"

"It's not what you've done. It's what you can do."

Beth shook her head, unable to imagine how she
could make up for the harm she'd caused. "I can only
make things worse."

"Beth, listen to me. There has always been an empty
place in my son's heart that only Monty could have
filled. I have urged him to no avail to go and meet his
father so that he can then get on with his life. Reese is
a compassionate and intelligent man, meant for so
much more than what he has settled for. Until you
came I thought he'd never have a chance at real happiness. He needs you, Beth. For the first time in his
life, he's stepped outside his superficial existence and
fallen in love. With you by his side he can begin to find
his way."

"No, Sylvie. It's too late for us."

"Too late? My dear, it's never too late to love."

"I don't believe he'll ever forgive me for betraying
him, for all those times I lied and deceived him. He
didn't hesitate to tell me how good I am at... those
things." She stopped and slowly brought her hand to
her mouth to cover her gasp. A short, sharp laugh
broke in her throat. "I have become very good at convincing people of things that aren't true." Lowering her
hand, she looked at Sylvie. "It's time to put my one
proven talent to a final test. And if it works..." She
paced the parquet floor, rubbing her temples, scowl-
ing in her attempt to concentrate, growling with frustration when she couldn't get it straight in her mind.

Then laughing out loud when she did. "Oh, Sylvie, if I can make it work..."

"Beth, if you can make what work? What are you going to do?"

Throwing her arms around the woman, she hugged her close, then hurried to the door. "You'll find out soon enough."

Ten

During the long drive down to the Riviera, Beth had plenty of time to concoct the outrageous lies she was going to tell Eugene. She rehearsed them ad nauseam, then prepared herself for every protest and stumbling block he would toss in her way. All of that didn't stop the bat-winged butterflies attacking her stomach as she stepped out of the Reese's "borrowed" Jaguar in front of the Cap Ferrat villa. Resting her fingers over her flat belly, she told herself to relax. And that the floaty sensation she was experiencing was simply a case of nerves. Wasn't it?

She leaned back against the car door as another possible explanation hit her. No, the idea was ridiculous. They'd been careless only one time. This couldn't be happening. Not with everything else caving in. She pushed away from the car and headed past the colonnade. After the emotions she'd been through a messed-up menstrual cycle was a predictable consequence. She had committed a terrible injustice against a man she had grown to love and rectifying that injustice was the only thing that should be concerning her now.

Maybe Reese would never forgive her, but at least she could spare him the glare of public scrutiny. And one day when he was ready to take a step closer to resolving his feelings for his father, he could do so on his own terms.

She allowed herself one final twinge of apprehension as she walked into the main salon. Eugene Sprague set his three-cherry Manhattan aside and jumped up from his chair. "Beth!" he said, giving her his best cat-about-to-eat-a-canary smirk while he strained for a look over her shoulder. "Where is he?"

"With his family," she said, tossing her purse on a chair. She crossed the room to the marble-topped bar and reached beneath it for a glass, then plunked in a few ice cubes. "His real family," she said, opening a bottle of mineral water and pouring herself a glassful. She didn't miss Eugene's stunned smile slowly disintegrate.

"Hold on," he said, waving his hand. "What do you mean—his real family?"

"Reese Marchand is not Harrison Montgomery's son."

He paused for a beat, then jutted his chin in her direction. "That's it? I'm supposed to accept that one-liner without any further explanation?"

Beth slammed her water glass on the bar and pointed at Eugene. "You want the details? You want to know how I ended up humiliating myself in front of that man and his family just because you didn't do your research?" Straightening her fingers, she flipped her hand palm up. "Well, why not? I lived through it twice today. A third time ought to be a piece of cake."

"Then cut me a big slice and get on with it, blondie."

"I asked Reese if Montgomery was his father and he laughed at me. At least, at first he laughed at me. When I told him why I was asking, he stopped laughing very quickly. And when I explained to him how the beginning of his mother's pregnancy fitted so conveniently into the time frame of Montgomery's foreign-service tour in Paris, he called me a string of names I'm not going to repeat . . . even for you."

Eugene pinched the corners of his mouth, then rocked impatiently on the balls of his feet. "And that's when you left?" he asked, his voice a deceptive monotone.

"No, that's when I should have left. But, you know me. I wasn't giving up that easily," she said, watching Eugene's too-slow nod. "I had to go ask his mother." She did a double take, then narrowed her eyes. "What's that look for? You didn't think, after what I put myself through this summer, I'd give up that easily?" she asked, snapping her fingers. "Did you?"

As Eugene's face clouded with the first signs of self-doubt, Beth continued. "Sylvie Marchand doesn't deny or even regret meeting Montgomery. She says they were never lovers because she was already betrothed to Philippe Marchand when she met him. She insists her only connection to Montgomery was through her cultural-affairs work within the diplomatic community." She rolled her eyes. "But I couldn't leave it at that. I had to drop a little lower on the food chain and suggest she could be making it all up. And that Montgomery could still be Reese's father."

Planting an elbow on the bar, Beth rubbed at her forehead. The vivid memories of what had really occurred at Château Beaumont earlier that day came into her mind. She pictured Reese, tripping his way at top speed through every emotion she could conceive of in reaction to her betrayal. Until that moment Reese had been quietly dealing with his private torment. How could she have allowed things to come to this?

"Beth, what did his mother say?"

When she looked at Eugene again she didn't have to fake a look of shame. Her body burned with it. "I have to give that lady a lot of credit," she said, lowering her head and shaking it. "Sylvie has poise and grace, the likes of which I have never seen."

He shrugged, spinning an uneven circle with his hand. "Whatever. Go on."

"When I told her I wanted proof, she took me into the library and showed me old photographs from her husband's side of the family." She took a drink, then slowly wiped her lips.

Eugene walked toward her, his eyes widening as he came closer. "And?"

"Reese is a dead ringer for a great uncle of his father's. I mean, right down to the shape of his ears and that patrician nose. And the resemblance he shares to a half-dozen others relatives on that side of his family is almost as strong." She produced what she hoped was a convincing shiver. "It was creepy."

Eugene's pupils were fixed and, Beth would swear, dilating from the impact of the lies she'd delivered.

"Get hold of yourself." She slapped him on the arm as she began to take her first deep breath in hours. "You'll survive." *And so will I. But without you, Reese, that's about all I expect to do.*

"Dammit," Eugene said, pounding both fists on the pink marble. "Dammit, dammit, dammit! All this time and money..." He fingered his lips as he shook his head and began to pace. "There's got to be a way to salvage something out of this fiasco. I can feel it...if I could just—"

"Give it up, Eugene," she said, even as she saw the gleam coming into his eyes. "It's over. I want no more part of it."

"I know," he said, as if he hadn't heard her. "I'll have those photos of you and Marchand at that outdoor restaurant published anyway. I'll drop in a mention about Montgomery once dating his mother. Any voting fool will be able to see the resemblance between Reese and Montgomery. I'll have them run the week before the election, when it will be too late for any effective damage control. That ought to buy us some votes. Mark my word, their spin doctors will be popping brain circuits over this." He turned toward her as she came out from behind the bar. "Phew! Didn't think I could pull a save out of that. What do you think?"

Walking up to him, she grabbed a handful of his silk shirtfront and leaned in. "No," she said. Softly. Deliberately.

"No? No what?"

"No more dirty tricks, Eugene. Enough is enough."

"Are you crazy?"

"To keep this up, I'd have to be. But I can't... keep...doing...this."

"You don't have to," he said, peeling her fingers from his shirt. "I will."

"No, you won't."

He gave a long, deep, impatient sigh. "Time for you to back away, Beth. I'll be taking over from here."

"I'm serious, Eugene. This project was a long shot to begin with and I'm going to regret it for the rest of my life. We've made the Marchands suffer for something that never happened. We're not going to hurt them any more."

He laughed. "*We're not?* And just how are we going to accomplish that?"

"Stop it. Or, I swear, the moment those photos hit the newsstands, I'll call a news conference of my own. And I'll implicate you and President Pierson."

"And how would you do that?"

"For starters, there's a paper trail back and forth across the Atlantic several times over and I'll be very happy to show it to every newspaper, every magazine show and everyone else who wants a look. You know, it all circles back to you."

"You'll go down with me—"

"I've already sunk as low as I can go."

"Hey," he said in that crooning tone she'd learned to despise. "Don't do this to me. To yourself. Remember what you wanted out of this? How are we going to see that that happens? Let me do this, Beth, and the outcome's guaranteed."

"Nothing in this life is guaranteed. It's time to do the decent thing. Let this man be."

"Come on, stick with the team. Keep your eye on that prize and we've got our victory," he said, standing his ground. "We win."

"Wrong" came a masculine voice from across the room. "You lose."

Both Beth and Eugene turned toward the open foyer door. And for one brilliant flash of a second, Beth didn't trust her eyes. She blinked, then forced herself to breathe, as she continued taking in the sight before her. Reese, his hair windblown, his smoky topaz eyes hard and unforgiving and his jaw set with steely determination. She'd seen him angry before, but this was a man in complete and formidable control. And she loved him with every fiber of her being for it.

Eugene turned fully to face him. "Reese Marchand."

"That's right," Reese said, never glancing at Beth. "Marchand." He moved into the room, his soft footfalls absorbed by the pale rug.

Her heart pounded with his every step. She should have known he'd follow her. And why shouldn't he? These minutes with Eugene were most likely to be the pivotal point in his life. She swallowed. And hers.

"You'd do well to listen to her," Reese said, indicating Beth with a flick of his thumb.

"Hold on a minute," Eugene said. "Maybe we could work something out. Something mutually beneficial to both of us."

As Beth's boss continued with a hastily concocted plan, Reese could hear her groan of disgust. For the first time since revealing what she'd been after all summer, he found himself considering just what kind of a man she'd had to deal with. Reese held up his hand for Eugene to stop. "I don't care who wins the election. I only care about the people I love, and I'll be damned if you'll hurt them anymore. So take some free advice. If your employee here thinks she can find a little redemption in closing the book on this, then I suggest you follow suit. Because if you don't, I'll be right beside her, defending my family by backing her case against you."

"You're bluffing."

"Are you willing to hang the rest of your career and possibly Tyler Pierson's reelection on proving that? Or are you going to pack it in and slither back to Washington?"

Eugene looked first at Reese and then at Beth, his confusion and frustration growing by the millisecond. "Are you two in on...?" He shook his head as if the rest of his question suddenly didn't matter anymore. Looking up at Reese, he bared his teeth through thinned lips and made an animal sound in the back of his throat. "You bastard!" Eugene started around him.

Reese's hand shot out, clamping around Eugene's shoulder and stopping him short in his tracks. "Wrong. Try again."

"Son of a—UHHHHH!"

Reese slammed him hard against the wall and held him there with both hands. "What were you going to say?"

"Okay! Okay! Marchand. Marchand."

"That's better," Reese said, releasing Eugene from his crushing grip, then helping him out of the room with a well-placed shove to the small of his back. When he was safely away from Reese, Eugene let out a string of equally disquieting curses, this time visiting them upon himself.

When Eugene finally slammed the door, Reese pulled in a breath, and vaguely wondered why he wasn't detecting the acrid after-smell of a bloody battle. Then he heard her coming up behind him and realized the real battle was about to begin. The one being fought between his heart and his head. She stopped even with him, keeping her distance by at least two yards.

"Reese?"

He turned his face toward her and waited while she gathered more courage to continue.

She cleared her throat, then looked him in the eye. He saw an unnamed fear there, but he also saw enough bravery to get her through whatever she was going to tell him. The word *survivor* came to his mind.

"You don't have to worry. Eugene won't let a word of this leak out." Struggling to keep her chin up, she started away from him.

"Hold on," he said, going after her. "Why did you leave Château Beaumont without telling me? And why did you tell your boss all those lies?"

"None of that is important," she said, keeping her back to him. "It only matters that you and your family don't have to worry about him taking this any further. And now you can begin to forget you ever met me."

She started away again, but his hand closed over her shoulder. This time, his grip contained just enough pressure to let her know they weren't through. When she turned to look at him, a hundred different messages and a thousand different questions were pouring out of her brandy-colored eyes. She'd never looked more beautiful, more desirable, more in need of his love than she did right now. It was his choice now. If he had any sense he'd let her walk away. But knowing Beth Langdon was never about good sense and safe choices.

"What do you want?" she asked.

The truth, he wanted to shout. *Every last syllable of it, so that with or without you, I can think about living again.* All his hours at the casino, all the chances he'd taken with his boat and his car and every other daredevil adventure he'd indulged himself with hadn't prepared him for this. The biggest gamble of his life. But if Beth Langdon and what they'd had together wasn't worth the risk, then nothing else would ever be again. And all because he couldn't deny that he still loved her.

"We have to talk, but not here in this place," he said. "Are you willing to come to my apartment?"

She looked up at him and he thought his heart had suddenly dissolved into his bloodstream. Every part of him was waiting, pulsing, aching for her answer.

"Yes."

She said nothing else during the drive back to Monaco, and neither did he until after he'd let them into his apartment and pushed open the balcony doors. "Out here okay with you?" he asked. She nodded and went ahead of him.

"We could always talk out here, couldn't we?" she asked after a few seconds. Her eyes darted nervously to and from his face. She slid her hand back and forth over the railing and coughed. "Isn't it late for fireworks? I thought they were always over by this time. All those beautiful colors rushing by..."

"What are you going to do now, Beth?"

She looked down at her fingers as they went still on the railing. "I'm going back to Washington and hand in my resignation. And then I'm getting myself as far away from that place as possible."

"Just like that, you're giving up your career, your plans, your life in that town?"

"Life? I never had a life there," she said, lifting her gaze to the explosions of color cascading over the harbor.

He watched a few coiling curls tumbling onto her forehead in a sudden breeze. She brushed them back.

"I see. So all those plans for a big, bright career there are gone? All your high-placed contacts down the drain?"

Her mouth opened in surprise. She stared at him, then shook her head. "You think I did this to you for some cushy job in Pierson's next administration, don't you?"

"Isn't that true?" he asked, his soft, even words delivering more of a challenge than anything else he could have said or done. *Tell me something else, Beth. Tell me anything other than it was greed or vanity or unchecked ambition that made you compromise yourself. And then let me go on loving you.*

She grabbed the railing and glared at him.

"You want to know why I did it? Because Eugene Sprague promised me that if President Pierson was reelected, the first thing he would do is get that bill for decent housing signed into law. He thought proof of Montgomery's...indiscretion would be enough to sink 'the keeper of the new morality' on election day." Brushing her hair away from her face, she looked away from him and held her head very still before she continued. "Maybe it sounds naive or even stupid, but I needed to believe that would happen," she said, measuring each word before she delivered it.

"Why was that bill so important?" he asked, more bewildered than he'd been ten hours ago.

"I...well, I had some very touching moments happen to me while I was doing volunteer work in a homeless shelter. I was in a position to listen to people's stories of how they ended up there. One family told me that the shock of losing their home was like experiencing a death. One day they had a roof over their head, a swing set in the backyard and—''

"Wait a minute," he said, cutting her off. "You're trying to tell me, because you volunteered a few hours in a soup kitchen, that you were so moved that you stooped into this mess?" He shook his head. "Beth, even with all your lies, I think I know you better than—''

She turned to him then, that soft, ethereal look changing to fire before his eyes. "You don't know anything about me," she said, slapping her palm on the railing.

He grabbed a portion of the railing next to her. "Then for God's sake tell me. After everything that's happened—''

"All right! When you assumed I'd had a perfectly charming childhood, you couldn't have been further from the truth. My life wasn't an endless round of pink-frosted birthday cakes and kittens in Christmas stockings," she said, slapping away a tear from her cheek. "All of that ended when my father suddenly lost his job and we lost our home."

"And he couldn't get another one?" he asked quietly as the first prickles of awareness closed around his heart.

"He tried so hard, but it just didn't happen and in one month our world fell in on us." She brushed more tears away with a quick swipe from both her hands. "Everything my parents worked for was gone."

A stunned silence followed the shock of her words. But not for long. "How bad did it get?"

She tried waving away his question as if it weren't important now. But it was more important than ever because it had to do with understanding this woman he'd never stopped loving. "Beth?" He dropped his voice to a gentle whisper. "You need to tell me all of it, because you need to say it and I need to hear it."

"All of it? I don't know if I want to remember all of it." She swallowed hard, then looked away from him. After a few seconds she turned her back on the glittering harbor with its million-dollar yachts, its twinkling skyline and the continuing explosions of colored light. Lifting her chin, she stared blindly into the apartment's interior. "We slept in our car for a month because we had no place else to go. I was seven years old."

He cursed under his breath.

"It was okay during the day when the shopping malls were open. But at night when we had to use the bathroom we had to drive around to different service stations. The trick was not to use the same place too often, because after a while they recognized us and wouldn't give us the key."

"My God, Beth," he said, taking her hands in his. "You were just a little girl."

She looked up at him. "Our relatives treated us as if we were their worst nightmare. And except for the homeless shelters that took us in when they had room, everyone else treated us as if we were dirt."

Pulling her hands from his, she balled them into fists. The defiant gesture tore at the roots of his heart.

"But we weren't dirty. We weren't," she said, as the tears flowed down her cheeks. "We washed ourselves every day."

He wanted to tell her that it was over. That everything was all right now. And that he would do anything it took so that she would never have to suffer those indignities again. But he couldn't talk over the

lump in his throat. Instead he took her in his arms and
rocked her as she wept and told him the rest.

"It seemed to go on that way forever, but then my
parents got full-time jobs and things started to get better. I worked hard and got myself a scholarship to
Northwestern. Once college was behind me, I was certain I could go down to Washington and help solve the
homeless problem. What an idiot I was to think that. I
kept on plugging, though. But by the time Eugene
came to me with this half-baked idea, I was so desperate I think I wanted him to convince me to do it." She
pressed her hands against his chest and lifted her face
to look at him. "Reese, I wanted this so badly to work
because nothing else I was doing was making a dent in
the problem."

He stroked her hair and nodded. "And because you
believed you could make a difference. You saw a
problem, but instead of waiting around for someone
else to solve it, you did what you thought best. At least,
at the time what you thought best."

His gentle words and soft touch calmed her enough
to think more clearly about what she'd told him. She'd
kept the memories of that humiliating time locked inside her for two decades. Why had she told him about
that shameful period of her life, when she couldn't
bring herself to talk about it with her family? Her face
was stinging with the embarrassment of him knowing.
Moving out of his embrace, she shoved her fingers
through her hair and looked anywhere but at him. "I
only told you so that you could understand. I don't
want your pity."

"Pity? Beth, I admire you. You weren't looking for
a thrill when you risked it all. You did it because you
believed you could make a difference."

"And I nearly brought you down because of it. I don't know what else to tell you before I go except that I'm deeply sorry for what I did." She got as far as the open door to the living room.

"What's your hurry? You have nothing to go back to."

"I know that," she said, trying her damnedest to sound brave and confident, when his words were killing her. "But I've started out with less than nothing before. And I'll do it again."

"Where will you go to do that?"

She shrugged. "It doesn't matter."

"Turn around, Beth."

For a terrifying moment, he thought she wouldn't. But he quickly came to his senses. Beth Langdon was the bravest person he knew; she'd faced more daunting situations than a look back at him. Hadn't she? "Beth?"

Holding on to the edge of the door, she slowly twisted around to look at him. "Yes?"

"It matters to me," he said.

"Does it?" she asked, her voice a dry whisper, her eyes filling with a glimmering of hope.

"What you're looking for is here," he said, as he started across the balcony to her. She met him halfway, melting into his embrace with a little cry. "You're home, Beth. We're both home."

"I love you—I love you so much," she said, as he buried his face in her hair and breathed in her sweet, familiar scent. "Forgive me. I should have told you—"

"And I should have told you," he said, glorying in the feel of her body pressed so closely to his. "No more secrets, Beth. No more lies."

"I swear it," she said as he covered her face in a flurry of kisses.

As the fireworks finale lit the sky above them, the percussion of each dazzling explosion was an echo of their heartbeats and a celebration of their love.

After a moment, she pulled back to look at him as if she had to make sure the moment was really happening. Her intense gaze reached inside him, claiming his heart in exchange for her own. "We *are* home."

He held back the curly blond tendrils stirring around her face in the evening breeze and nodded. "I love you, Beth. Whatever you want. Whatever you need. It's yours. Just ask."

Sliding her thumb along his cheekbone, she caressed his face. "Make love to me, Reese."

He smiled. One of those big, wonderful smiles that made his eyes crinkle at their corners and her heart leap with happiness. "*Mon ange polisson,* I've been making love to you since the moment I first saw you."

She gave a nervous laugh as she wiped the last of her tears from her face. "Well, no wonder I feel so tingly whenever you're around."

He picked her up in his arms and took her to his bedroom. She was already unbuttoning his shirt as he lowered her feet to the floor. In a matter of seconds they were naked and she was back in his arms. "Don't leave me, Beth," he whispered as he laid her on the white bedspread and began to bathe her in his healing love.

"Never," she whispered back, as he continued kissing her. Every inch of her. Her hurried breathing turned into a moan when kissing wasn't enough. "Whatever you want. Whatever you need." But this time, she didn't have to ask.

"I know," he whispered fervently, as he parted her thighs. "I know." Entering her in one sure stroke, he took her shiver of anticipation and, fulfilling the promise he made with his eyes, turned it into the purist, richest pleasure they'd ever known.

Much later, when he'd pulled on his trousers and she'd slipped into his robe, they went back out onto the balcony. As she stood at the rail he wrapped himself around her. For a long time they stood quietly in the velvet darkness, absorbing the splendor of their moment.

"Shall I make it formal?" he whispered.

She looked back at him and smiled. "Whatever pleases you."

With his heart beating wildly, he took her hands in his and went down on one knee. For a few seconds all he could manage to do was drink in her luminous beauty. The robe she wore had slipped off one shoulder and her hair was making a lacy gold curtain against the dark night. Her smile was heavenly, but what else could he expect from his naughty angel? "You please me, Beth. And if you let me, I'll spend the rest of my life showing you just how much. Will you marry me?"

Leaning her face close to his, she filled his heart with a glimpse of the future. Golden, loving and infinitely theirs.

"I will," she whispered.

Epilogue

"There you are, Mrs. Marchand," Reese said as Beth came down the path into the back garden of the olive-mill house. "How did your meeting go?"

She smiled a secret smile as she dropped her packages on the patio table and went into his arms. "You'll be proud to know that the Creighton-Lee Foundation has accepted your wife's offer to work with their homeless project."

"Very proud. I hope they know what a dedicated worker they're getting."

She rubbed noses with him, then let him capture her lips in a playful kiss. "Mmmmmmm. Sorry I took so long, but I had a few more stops to make while I was in Nice." Before he could ask her about them, she hurriedly changed the subject. "Did Sylvie and Philippe call yet?"

"Yes. They won't be arriving until at least seven," he said, before he began stringing kisses down her neck. "That gives us at least five hours to—"

"Make sure I'm ready for my in-laws' first visit."

He quickly raised his head to give her a challenging stare. "Beth..." he said, his voice a comical warning.

Smiling again, she traced his bottom lip with her fingertip. "But I think I could be persuaded to put aside the dust cloth and celebrate our anniversary. One whole month today," she said, as he gently swayed her in the circle of his arms. The scents of fresh herbs and upturned earth filled the warm air, along with the sound of the cicadas. "What have you been doing all day?"

"I spent most of it working in the garden. We have a major problem with the cilantro. It's out of control and—"

She didn't even try to stop her throaty giggle. "Are you sure you're going to be able to handle all this domestic tranquillity?"

He laughed along with her, until the sparkle in his eyes softened to a glow. "Before you came into my life, I never knew happiness like this existed. I had about as much direction as a roulette wheel. I was spinning in circles, going nowhere fast." He watched her face a moment, then flexed his knees to level his eyes to hers. "Beth?"

She ruffled his already tousled hair. "Sorry," she said, swallowing her tears as she backed out of his arms. "I know I've been a little emotional lately." She shrugged. "But some people just cry when they're happy."

Resting his hands on his lean, jeaned hips, he pretended to give her a severe sizing up. The attempt failed beautifully when he chuckled and drew her back into his arms for a quick kiss. "Come on. I've got something in the house to show you," he said, reaching for her packages. "We'll see how happy you are then."

"Sounds intriguing. Do I get a hint?" she said, following him to the door, then opening it for them.

"It's an anniversary present from my mother. She and Philippe would have brought it down in the car with them," he said, plunking her packages on the kitchen table. "But it needed special packing and shipping." He took her hand and led her through the archway to the living room. "I had the deliverymen help me hang it when they were here this morning. Let's see if you like it any better than the first time you saw it."

Beth stopped just inside the living room. "The tapestry Sylvie wanted to give us. Oh, Reese, I liked it first time I saw it. I just had, well ... other things on my mind that day." She stepped up close to it to study the fine detail of the piece. "It's perfect right here by the staircase. Don't you think?"

Nodding, Reese walked over and wrapped his arm around her shoulders. "My mother told me something else about it."

"What was that?" she asked, sensing by his serious tone that he'd been deeply affected by the conversation. She waited, turning her full attention to Reese. And then a thought came into her mind. "This has something to do with Montgomery, doesn't it?"

"Married four weeks," he announced goodnaturedly "and already she's reading my mind." He looked at her and then back at the woodland scene. "Montgomery bought the tapestry for my mother."

Beth nodded slowly. "And now it hangs in your house. Are you okay with that?"

"In our house," he corrected as the wall clock chimed the hour. "And because it's in *our* house I am okay with that," he said, turning away from the tapestry. He walked over to the antique armoire and opened the carved doors. "We can talk about that later. In the meantime, I know you don't like to miss the news," he said, rolling out the TV shelf. He handed her the remote. "Are you hungry?"

She nodded. "I skipped lunch."

"Have a seat. I'll bring something in," he said, as he headed toward the kitchen.

"Reese?"

He braced his hand on the soft-colored stone wall and turned. Their gazes connected instantly. "I know. 'Don't forget the strawberries.' Right?"

Kicking off her shoes, she plopped onto the sofa and crossed her arms on an oversized throw pillow in its corner. "I love you." Before he disappeared into the kitchen she saw the growing smile on his face. His obvious contentment with their new life made her stomach flutter.

As she twisted around on the pillow, she caught a glimpse of the tapestry from the corner of her eye. Lowering the remote to her lap, she stared at the richly woven wall hanging. Surely Reese's acceptance of the tapestry was a sign that he was getting closer to dealing with the unfinished business between Montgomery and him. And when he was finally ready to make his move, she would be at his side.

Pointing the remote control at the TV, she clicked the button, and as if by the power of her own thoughts, Harrison Montgomery's face appeared. The picture segued into a report about Dara Seabrook, Montgomery's goddaughter. She had just finished a speech that was bringing thunderous applause from her audience of university students. As the brunette beauty headed back to a stretch limo she turned to wave and the camera went in for a close-up.

"Dara Seabrook," Reese said, sliding a tray onto the coffee table in front of the sofa. He handed Beth a glass of mineral water. "Quite a secret weapon. Looks and brains and total loyalty. They say she could win the election for my father."

Beth set her water glass aside as her gaze narrowed on her husband's profile. He'd just referred to Harrison Montgomery as his father and was now casually smearing Brie onto a piece of crusty French bread. What else could possibly happen today that would surprise her more? Her gaze wandered back to the TV screen.

A second later a peculiar sensation zipped up her spine when she noticed the man next to Dara. The dark-haired stranger removed his sunglasses and Beth felt her heart take an extra beat. If she didn't know any better, she could swear she was looking at Reese's eyes. She leaned forward for a closer look, then blinked twice. Every day and night since their wedding, she'd been doing a lot of looking into Reese's eyes. And Harrison Montgomery's picture was just on the screen a few minutes ago. Those two facts plus this handsome stranger's mild resemblance had to be the reasons for her reaction. Right?

"Reese? Do you know who this man is next to Dara?"

He looked up a second after the picture changed back to the anchorwoman. "Sorry, I missed him." Reese offered her a piece of crusty bread smeared with a healthy dollop of Brie. "Are you okay. You look a little pale."

"I...I'm fine," she said, not wanting to dwell on the eerie feeling. She waved off the bread. "No, thanks."

He looked at the bread, then set it down. "Beth, are you still upset about yesterday's newscast when President Pierson's press secretary announced he was planning to veto that housing bill when it came across his desk?"

She swallowed as she clicked off the remote and set it on the table. "I was upset when I heard," she said, picking up the bowl of strawberries. "But this is an election year and things have a way of sorting themselves out when you least expect them to."

Lifting a berry from the bowl, she smiled at her husband before biting into the fruit. Before she swallowed, she was reaching for another. "I feel very positive about working with the Creighton-Lee Foundation. I can do a lot of good hands-on work there."

He nodded, then pointed to her bowl of berries. "I don't know what you're going to do when those strawberry plants near the olive grove stop producing. Lately you've been downing those things as if they were potato chips."

Beth stared at the next strawberry she'd poised at her lips. "I know wild strawberries are rare. And hard to find," she said, teasing him with his own words. "But they're sweet. So sweet they make me ache, and still I go back for more."

"It's true," he said, setting the bowl aside then running his hand over her hip. "After one taste, nothing else will ever be quite so satisfying."

She held the fruit to his lips, and for a moment he looked as if he couldn't decide if he wanted it or not. With a sudden growl, he rushed forward, pushing her back on the gold-tasseled pillows. He captured the berry between his lips, and when it looked as if he would suck it into his mouth, he leaned close. She took a nibble. And then another. The playful move turned into a strawberry-flavored kiss that left her appetite for Reese anything but sated.

"Before this gets out of hand," he said, reaching for a folded paper he'd brought in on the tray, "happy anniversary."

Unfolding the paper, she scanned the fax, doing her best to translate it into English. "Reese, all I understand is Air France."

"It's a confirmation of flight reservations."

"For me?"

"For us. I thought next month would be a good time to visit your parents and your sister. That one week we had them over for the wedding was hectic. I also wanted us to go out to California to see Duncan. It's time he and I have a talk about the champagne business."

"Thank you, this is a wonderful surprise!" she whispered, hugging him close for a long moment. Moving back, she brushed at her eyes. "Reese? Is there another reason?"

He hesitated, then leaned back on the sofa. For a long time he said nothing, then he rubbed his mouth and began. ''I used to be known as something of a daredevil. Afraid of nothing. Willing to try anything. But deep down where it counted, I feared the one thing I was never willing to face.'' He reached for Beth's hand and pressed it to the center of his chest. ''But this month with you has opened up a whole new part of me. I don't know what's going to happen over there, but something tells me if I'm ever going to find any peace with Montgomery, I'm going to have to go back to the States to do it.''

''Whatever happens,'' she said, ''you won't be alone.''

''How did I get so lucky?'' He lifted her hand to kiss her palm. ''You're absolutely radiant. Do you get more beautiful every day, or do I just love you more every day?''

The moment swelled with love and she could hardly speak when she opened her mouth. ''I have a gift for you, too.''

He gave her cheek a light caress, then began sliding his hand down her soft curves. When his hand was resting on the flat plane of her belly, he leaned in to kiss her. ''Where is it?''

She closed her hand over his. ''You're holding it. Or him. Or her. We won't know for certain until May.'' She studied his stunned expression and hurried on. ''It happened the afternoon you first brought me here. Remember?'' She smiled as he lifted his hand from her, then placed it there again as if it were all too much to believe. ''When we decided . . .''

"To risk it all," he said, his poignant expression filling her with more love than she'd ever known. Love for him. For them. And now for the new life growing inside her.

"I love you, Beth."

"I love you, too," she said, and as he took her in his tender embrace, she thought she heard his heart mend a little more.

* * * * *

Don't miss the exciting third book in the
SONS AND LOVERS *trilogy,*
RIDGE: THE AVENGER by Leanne Banks—
coming next month from Silhouette Desire.

COMING NEXT MONTH

**#985 THE BEAUTY, THE BEAST AND THE BABY—
Dixie Browning**

Tall, Dark and Handsome
March's *Man of the Month*, gorgeous Gus Wydowski, didn't
need anyone—especially a beautiful woman with a baby. But
Mariah Brady soon had him longing for a family to call his own....

#986 THE LAST GROOM ON EARTH—Kristin James

Angela Hewitt vowed she'd never fall for sexy Bryce Richards's
charm—even if he were the last man on earth. But when he came
to her rescue, falling for Bryce was the *least* of her troubles....

#987 RIDGE: THE AVENGER—Leanne Banks

Sons and Lovers
It was bad enough Ridge Jackson was hired to protect feisty
Dara Seabrook—now he was finding it impossible to resist her!
Ridge could have any woman he wanted; why then did he want
Dara, the one woman who might never be his?

#988 HUSBAND: OPTIONAL—Marie Ferrarella

The Baby of the Month Club
When Jackson Cain returned to town, he was shocked to discover
a very pregnant Mallory Flannigan. And though she claimed the
child wasn't his, Jackson was sure she was hiding something!

#989 ZOE AND THE BEST MAN—Carole Buck

Wedding Belles
Zoe Armitage wanted a husband and kids, not a rugged bachelor
who'd never settle down! Gabriel Flynn stole her heart, but would
he ever abandon his wandering ways to make Zoe his wife?

#990 JUST A MEMORY AWAY—Helen R. Myers

Free-spirited Frankie Jones was crazy about the mysterious man
she found suffering from amnesia. But once he discovered his
true identity, would he hightail it out of town for good?

Take 4 bestselling love stories FREE

Plus get a FREE surprise gift!

Bestselling author

RACHEL LEE

takes her Conard County series to new heights with

A CONARD COUNTY Reckoning

This March, Rachel Lee brings readers a brand-new, longer-length, out-of-series title featuring the characters from her successful Conard County miniseries.

Janet Tate and Abel Pierce have both been betrayed and carry deep, bitter memories. Brought together by great passion, they must learn to trust again.

"Conard County is a wonderful place to visit! Rachel Lee has crafted warm, enchanting stories. These are wonderful books to curl up with and read. I highly recommend them."
—*New York Times* bestselling author
Heather Graham Pozzessere

Available in March, wherever Silhouette books are sold.

Are your lips succulent, impetuous, delicious or racy?

Find out in a very special Valentine's Day promotion—THAT SPECIAL KISS!

Inside four special Harlequin and Silhouette February books are details for THAT SPECIAL KISS! explaining how you can have your lip prints read by a romance expert.

Look for details in the following series books, written by four of Harlequin and Silhouette readers' favorite authors:

Silhouette Intimate Moments #691
Mackenzie's Pleasure by *New York Times* bestselling author Linda Howard

Harlequin Romance #3395
Because of the Baby by Debbie Macomber

Silhouette Desire #979
Megan's Marriage by Annette Broadrick

Harlequin Presents #1793
The One and Only by Carole Mortimer

Fun, romance, four top-selling authors, plus a **FREE** gift! This is a very special Valentine's Day you won't want to miss! Only from Harlequin and Silhouette.

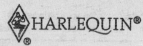

As seen on TV!

Free Gift Offer

With a Free Gift proof-of-purchase from any Silhouette® book,
you can receive a beautiful cubic zirconia pendant.

This gorgeous marquise-shaped stone is a genuine cubic
zirconia—accented by an 18" gold tone necklace.
(Approximate retail value $19.95)

Send for yours today...
compliments of ▼ *Silhouette*®
TM

To receive your free gift, a cubic zirconia pendant, send us one original proof-of-
purchase, photocopies not accepted, from the back of any Silhouette Romance™,
Silhouette Desire®, Silhouette Special Edition®, Silhouette Intimate Moments®
or Silhouette Shadows™ title available in February, March or April at your favorite
retail outlet, together with the Free Gift Certificate, plus a check or money order for
$1.75 U.S./$2.25 CAN. (do not send cash) to cover postage and handling, payable
to Silhouette Free Gift Offer. We will send you the specified gift. Allow 6 to 8 weeks for
delivery. Offer good until April 30, 1996 or while quantities last. Offer valid in the U.S. and
Canada only.

Free Gift Certificate

Name: _____

Address: _____

City: _____ State/Province: _____ Zip/Postal Code: _____

Mail this certificate, one proof-of-purchase and a check or money order for postage
and handling to: SILHOUETTE FREE GIFT OFFER 1996. In the U.S.: 3010 Walden
Avenue, P.O. Box 9057, Buffalo NY 14269-9057. In Canada: P.O. Box 622, Fort Erie,

---

FREE GIFT OFFER   079-KBZ-R
ONE PROOF-OF-PURCHASE
To collect your fabulous FREE GIFT, a cubic zirconia pendant, you must include this
original proof-of-purchase for each gift with the properly completed Free Gift Certificate.

079-KBZ-R

SILHOUETTE®
Desire®
CELEBRATION 1000

is on its way
in April, May and June 1996!

Join us for the celebration of Desire's 1000th book!
We'll have

- Book #1000, *Man of Ice* by Diana Palmer in May!
- Best-loved miniseries such as **Hawk's Way** by Joan Johnston, and **Daughters of Texas** by Annette Broadrick
- Fabulous new writers in our Debut author program, where you can collect <u>double</u> Pages and Privileges Proofs of Purchase

Plus you can enter our exciting Sweepstakes for a chance to win a beautiful piece of original Silhouette Desire cover art or one of many autographed Silhouette Desire books!

SILHOUETTE DESIRE'S CELEBRATION 1000
...because the best is yet to come!

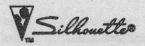